I didn't want to be interested in Romeo. I was swearing off guys.

Still, as I sat in my lifeguard chair, I kept looking back toward the sand-covered deck. Eventually I noticed that Whitney had left. The next time I looked over, I saw Romeo wading into the water. He really was in shape. His strides were long.

The waves hadn't started up yet, but I wasn't supposed to be watching cuties wading into the water. For one thing, that end of the pool wasn't my zone. For another, looking at him made my heart do this crazy dance. Distracting, very distracting.

MAKING A
SPLASH,
Caitlin

JADE PARKER

Point

ISBN-13: 978-0-545-04541-4
ISBN-10: 0-545-04541-X

12 11 10 9 8 7 6 5 4 3 2 1   8 9 10 11 12 13/0

Printed in the U.S.A.
First printing, June 2008

Book design by Steve Scott

CHAPTER ONE

It was disgusting. My brother kissing my best friend. Not that they were kissing right that minute — because Sean was driving. But I knew he *had* kissed Robyn. I hadn't wanted details. It was just a little too weird to even think about — my best friend and my brother.

How had *that* even happened — them getting together? Right under my nose?

How could Robyn not realize he was evil?

Worst of all? Now *I* had to sit in the backseat every morning as Sean drove us to the Paradise Falls water park. We all worked there, in different positions. Sean had started out the summer as a supervisor. Now he was working as a marketing assistant in the front offices. Robyn was a ride attendant in the kiddie area, officially known as Mini Falls. I was a lifeguard at Tsunami, the most awesome pool at Paradise Falls.

And okay, at the beginning of the summer, Sean had been Robyn's supervisor and they'd seen a lot of each other while working together, but still. Being around him all the time should have convinced her that she *didn't* want to be around him all the time. But that didn't happen, and I just didn't understand it. She'd always been dependable, the one with the most common sense. She wanted a geological reading of what was beneath the surface before diving in. Me? I just jumped into the water with complete faith that it was safe. Maybe that was the reason she now had a boyfriend and I had a broken heart.

I didn't want to think about that, so I concentrated on solving my daily su doku puzzle. Why couldn't boys be as easy to understand? I guess because they didn't come with little boxes that had only one solution.

I started to get nauseous. I rolled down the window, felt the breeze riffling through my black hair. At the beginning of the summer, I'd gotten it cut pretty short so all I had to do was run my fingers through it and every strand fell into place.

"Hey," Sean growled. "I'm running the air conditioning here."

His hair was as dark as mine, his eyes as blue. That was all we had in common — two things we'd inherited from our dad. Sean was tall, I was short. He was slender and could eat anything he wanted. I ate sweets only on holidays. Thank goodness, the Fourth of July was just around the corner. I even had some obscure holidays marked on my calendar to get me through when well-known holidays weren't close together — but I used them only in an emergency.

I wasn't chubby, but I didn't shop in the

petite section either. I was well-rounded, but then most of the women in my family were: my mom, my grandma, my aunts. "Sturdy stock" is how my dad referred to us, which sort of made us sound like cows with a questionable future. I loved Dad but he didn't believe in sugarcoating things. I liked things sugarcoated, which could be the reason that I was sturdy.

"I'm feeling carsick," I told Sean. Not that he would care. When we were little, he was always telling me gross stuff to make me feel sick. I think it was a brother thing.

Robyn twisted around and looked at me, her brown eyes filled with worry. A month ago, I'd been the one contorting around in the front seat so I could talk to her. A month ago, the summer had been filled with promise. Now it was just filled with long, hot days.

"Do you need him to pull over?" Robyn asked, holding her ponytail so the wind didn't whip her long, golden-brown hair around her face. She had some naturally light strands as though her hair couldn't decide if it should be blond or brown. But most of it was brown.

"I'm on the expressway," Sean said as though we didn't have sense enough to notice where we were.

"But if she's feeling bad —"

"Do I need to pull over?" he asked. "Let me know *now* because there's an exit ramp —"

How did Robyn even do that? How did she make Sean do stuff, pretend to be human? Before she came along he would have just told me to hang my head out the window like a dog.

"No, I'm fine." I rolled up the window. I just wanted to get to work as quickly as possible and out of the car. I felt as though I was suffocating, that tears were going to be squeezed out of my eyes at any moment. I wasn't normally so grumpy or so emotional, but getting my heart broken had really messed me up.

Robyn smiled, a smile she was giving me

a lot lately. A smile that said, "See, he's not mean. Not really."

I just so didn't get it. Her and him. I wanted her to be happy. I really did. But not with my brother.

Okay, so I wasn't adjusting well to them getting together. It was simply too weird. It would be like Cristina Yang on *Grey's Anatomy* suddenly getting together with McDreamy. Not that Sean was McDreamy, but Robyn was acting as though he was.

Oh, all right. Sean has never really done anything *mean*. Not really. It's just that he's my brother, he's older, and he thinks he knows *everything*. It doesn't help when I'm assigned to a teacher who also had Sean, because then I get to hear about how smart and creative he is. I'm smart, too. I just don't see a need to prove it by acing exams. I'm perfectly happy with what my dad calls "a respectable B."

To top it all off, now my best friend thought Sean was totally awesome. I wanted to gag whenever she started talking about how nice he was and how he looked out for people.

I thought Sean would never pull into the water park's parking lot. It was huge. Large enough to hold a few thousand cars. The water park was all about customer service, and that service began before any of us actually clocked in. It began when we took the parking slots farthest from the ticket booths. But we were young, in shape, and arrived before the sun was at its hottest so it was nothing for us to trudge across the asphalt.

Before Sean even brought the car to a complete stop, I opened the door, hopped out, and headed toward the entrance. I didn't want to watch them holding hands and walking along, bumping shoulders as though holding hands wasn't enough contact. Behind me, I heard two car doors slam shut.

"What's your hurry?" Sean asked.

I turned around, walking backward. "We're late. Maybe marketing assistants don't have to be on time, but us lowly peons do."

He'd put a spell over someone to get the supervisor's job. He had that power. Look what he'd done to Robyn. Now he had a job in the front offices that was even better.

This summer was the first that Robyn and I had worked here. It was Sean's third year, so *maybe* he *did* have the experience to be in charge. He was seventeen, two years older than Robyn and me.

Since I'd grown up with him believing he was the boss of me, I sometimes got a little irritated that now he *actually* was the boss of me. Even though he was no longer a supervisor, he was still in a position of authority.

I got to the employee gate, not paying much attention to the thousand or so people lined up at the ticket windows waiting for the park to open for the day, and swiped my employee badge through the electronic card reader. The gate clanked, signaling it had unlocked. I pushed it open. A guard stood on the other side. We had a lot of security here: guards at every entrance, guards who patrolled, security cameras. We were pretty high-tech.

"Hey, Caitlin," the guard said. He was shaped like a panda bear, big and cuddly, his round belly straining the buttons on his shirt. He was white-haired and had retired from some real job. I didn't think he'd be able to chase anyone down, which was probably the reason that he guarded the employee entrance. We followed the park rules. "No running" was our mantra.

"Good morning, Mr. Smith." I hurried past him to the path that led to the main part of the park, which meant walking by the park's mascot.

"*Brawk!* Welcome to Paradise Falls! *Brawk!*" The green-and-yellow parrot greeted everyone who walked by.

Before I worked here, I spent a good deal of my summers playing at the park. It had shade trees and palm trees and a real island theme going. Several areas of the park were covered in sand that was at least twelve inches deep so kids could build sand castles or just dig around.

I arrived at the grass hutlike employee locker room, pushed open the door, and walked to my locker. Several girls were there already, changing into their uniforms, talking, laughing. It was usually a pretty friendly place.

Beside my locker, a girl with blond hair that had amazing highlights was tucking her white polo shirt with the Paradise Falls logo into her red shorts. Employees who had long hair were supposed to wear it in a ponytail, but no one ever got after Whitney about her hair. They didn't get after her about anything, really. She said it was because she was so adorable. But I wasn't buying it.

"Hi, Whitney."

Robyn and I had met her at the beginning of the summer. She'd started out working with Robyn at Splash, a pretty boring slide in Mini Falls. Now Whitney worked in parties and entertainment. A lot of people reserved space for birthday parties or family reunions. The park also arranged special entertainment for certain occasions — like the upcoming Fourth of July.

"How's it going?" Whitney asked.

"Fine." I didn't know her well enough to unload on her, and now that I was out of the car, I was feeling better about things.

Underneath my clothes, I was wearing the park's official lifeguard uniform — a red tank bathing suit. It saved me a little time in the getting-ready department after I got to work. I took off my shorts and T-shirt.

"Are you going to have lunch with us today?" I asked.

"I'm going to try. We have three birthday parties scheduled for this morning."

"Sounds like fun." I almost sounded sincere.

"It's more fun than standing around watching people swim."

"I don't usually stand," I told her. "I sit."

"Whatever."

It wasn't that I didn't like her, but there was something about her that I didn't trust.

I couldn't explain it. She didn't look or act like someone who needed to work. She said she was working because her dad wanted her to. Although she didn't really seem to understand the meaning of the word "work." When she first started working with Robyn, Whitney didn't do anything except *work* on her *tan*. Now she seemed to be into assisting with the parties, so her attitude had improved a little. Although I had a sneaking suspicion that she told people what to do rather than doing it herself. She wasn't exactly a hands-on kind of girl.

I entered the code into the lock, opened the metal door, and tossed my clothes and beach bag — with my lunch — into the locker.

Whitney came a little closer. "So how is it with Robyn dating your brother? Used to it yet?"

"Weird and not really." I never understood people asking questions one right after the other.

"She really likes him," Whitney said.

"Well, obviously, otherwise she wouldn't be seeing him." I shook my head. "I had to stop listening to his phone conversations though. It was one thing to spy on my brother, but it seems totally wrong to spy on my best friend."

I'd developed a habit of standing and listening outside his bedroom door, because he had a deep voice and I could always hear him when he talked on his phone. I picked up some good gossip about people and happenings that way. But when Robyn was on the other end of his phone conversation — well, I just couldn't bring myself to eavesdrop.

"You really don't like not knowing the scoop on everything, do you?" Whitney asked.

"I really don't. Speaking of which, what's your deep, dark secret?"

She laughed. "What makes you think I have one?"

"Come on. Everything you own has a designer label on it, so why are you working at a water park?"

"Because it's so much fun to bug people like you."

She walked away without saying anything else. She and I had this real love-hate relationship going. It was strange because I actually enjoyed bantering with her. Robyn usually just followed along with whatever I wanted to do. Whitney challenged me.

Besides, Robyn liked Whitney so I was okay with her hanging around with us, although it had bothered me at first. Robyn and I had always been a clique of two — ever since we'd met in kindergarten. I'd always preferred it that way. I was more about quality than quantity. One good friend whom I trusted with everything was better than a lot of friends whom I knew just a little.

I heard Whitney say hi to someone. I looked over my shoulder. She was talking to Robyn. I returned my attention to getting ready. I clipped my badge onto the side of my red hip-pack and grabbed my whistle from the hook where I'd left it the day before. I dropped the lanyard over my head, draped it around my neck, and felt the weight of the metal whistle hit my chest.

"Are you okay?" Robyn asked.

I jumped, startled by her sudden nearness. I hated that she'd sneaked up on me. Even though I'd known she was in the area, I hadn't expected her to be by my side so quickly.

"You do realize he's evil."

She smiled as though I was silly. The dynamics of our relationship had changed once she started dating my brother. She didn't always believe everything I said.

"He's nice." She opened her locker.

"Just don't come crying to me when he hurts you."

"You don't mean that."

No, I didn't. I was there for her. I always would be. It's what best friends did.

"I just don't get why you like him so much."

"I know, but you don't have to."

It was as though his being older was rubbing off on her or something. She used to be really shy, kind of quiet. Now she was confident about everything.

Although maybe it wasn't him at all. Maybe it was the fact that she'd saved a kid who'd almost drowned.

That was supposed to be my job — as a lifeguard. So far, all I'd done this summer was blow my whistle when kids ran around the pool or didn't follow the rules that were posted.

"Are we okay?" Robyn asked.

"Yeah, totally." I adjusted my red Paradise Falls visor. Another part of our uniform. I slipped off my sparkly flip-flops, popped them in my locker, slammed it closed, and reset the lock. "Gotta go."

"Don't forget what Mr. T says."

Mr. T was the park's general manager. Supposedly his name was unpronounceable so he just went by "Mr. T." Robyn and I pointed our fingers at each other, the way

Mr. T did whenever he saw a park employee. "Be watchful out there!" we both said dramatically.

Then we laughed. It always felt good to laugh with Robyn. The problem was that these days she was mostly laughing with Sean. And I was laughing alone.

CHAPTER TWO

I was sitting in the lifeguard tower at the five-foot mark. Tsunami was twelve feet deep at the end of the pool farthest away from the Tsunami lounging deck. A huge wall was at the back end. Behind it were all the machines that created the awesome eight-foot waves. The alarm sounded to warn swimmers that the calm pool was about to transform and pretty soon the rippling waves would be heading toward shore. Tsunami was the cornerstone of the park. It was the largest pool, had the largest lounging deck, and the biggest pavilion. Around the outskirts, it had private cabanas for rent if people didn't want to mingle with the masses.

I didn't understand why anyone would come here for privacy.

I heard a girl release a high-pitched scream. It would take the waves a while to hit their maximum height, so right now they were just undulating around people. It could be scary if you were a kid and had never experienced it before.

But she wasn't a kid. She was probably my age. Blond. She was wearing a black string bikini and sitting on a guy's shoulders. He was so darkly tanned that I knew he loved being in the sun. I could relate. But I also had a job to do and since he was in my watch zone, I blew my whistle.

He turned around, looking all innocent. He was a true cutie. His wet black hair fell into his eyes. He flicked it back with a jerk of his head, his hands holding the girl's legs so she didn't go tumbling off.

"No carrying people on your shoulders!" I yelled.

"What?"

I didn't know if he hadn't heard me or he was just giving me a hard time. Lots of times people pretended not to hear us when we yelled at them, so I went into hand-signal mode. I made a motion to indicate the waves were starting up, made a motion of lifting something off my shoulders. "Put her down."

Even with her sitting on his broad shoulders, he managed to shrug. "Why?"

I pointed to the huge sign behind me where large letters proclaimed NO STANDING ON SHOULDERS.

Although she wasn't technically standing, it was still too dangerous. I was sure they'd done studies. Or someone had gotten hurt and sued the park. Rules were put in place for a reason.

"Give me a break," the guy yelled. "I'm strong."

Did he think I was blind and couldn't see that he was in shape? But it didn't matter how strong he was. Or how cute.

"It's the rules," I called out.

"Rules are made to be broken!"

"Do it or you're outta there."

He grinned at me. It was a challenging grin. I tried not to notice that it made him look even cuter. I wasn't being paid to notice cuteness factors, but it was a little hard not to notice.

"Do it!" I repeated with authority.

He sank below the water.

The girl screamed, "Romeo!"

Was that the guy's name? Who named their kid Romeo? Or was it what he told people his name was because he thought he was such hot stuff?

The girl shrieked again before she started swimming into the waves. He broke through to the surface and followed her.

I tried not to watch how powerfully he swam. I wasn't going to get sucked into crushing mode by good looks or an athletic build. I wasn't going to fall for a guy just because on a scale of one to ten, he was a twelve.

Romeo. Such a stupid name.

Of course, lately I thought all guys were lame, so it might not have mattered what his name was.

When I first started working here, I'd crushed on one of the other Tsunami life-guards — Tanner. He was blond and in shape. He'd come over to talk to me every now and then so I'd mistakenly thought he was crushing back. We'd hung out some, watched fireworks together, gone to a party, held hands, so I'd believed that he liked me as much as I liked him.

Then I'd caught him kissing a girl who worked in one of the souvenir shops. I didn't know her name, but I'd seen her when I walked through the shops area of the park. And I'd definitely seen her when he was kissing her.

When I'd confronted him, with her standing right there, he'd acted as innocent as Romeo had a few minutes earlier. *What? Me being bad?*

Guys could be such jerks.

Standing at the shallow edge of the pool now, where the waves rolled around his ankles, Tanner held his rescue tube against his side. He was definitely cute. He had blond hair that hung straight down past his ears. He looked like someone who did a lot of surfing — or would if we had a real beach nearby. He had more freckles on his shoulders now than he had at the beginning of summer. He was also more tanned, but then we all were. He was tall. During the school year, he played football.

During the summer, he apparently played with girls' hearts.

I hadn't seen him with Souvenir Chick since that fateful night when I'd caught them in a lip-lock, but the damage was done. I couldn't trust him, so I'd started ignoring him. Robyn had warned me early on that I shouldn't be interested in someone I worked with — that it would be hard to see him every day if things didn't work out. At the time, I'd been unable to imagine things not working out. But they hadn't, and she was right. It was hard to see him and be reminded again that I'd been a total fool. I'd never had a boyfriend. Had never even been kissed. I'd believed Tanner was the *one*, the one who would give me my first kiss. But it hadn't worked out that way.

It still stung — a couple of weeks after his betrayal.

I looked past him to the sand-covered Tsunami deck where the lounge chairs and occasional umbrella-covered tables were filled with guests. Behind that was the pavilion with picnic tables. It, too, was crowded with people. Summer was in full swing. Everyone was here for a good time.

I let my gaze wander over the guests frolicking in the pool. The waves ran for twelve minutes. Then they'd settle into calmness to give people a chance to catch their breath and the lifeguards a chance to make sure everyone was all right.

I stood up, holding my own red rescue tube against my stomach. I'd never really considered how boring it was to watch other

people having fun. I'd much rather be rushing up Thrill Hill where the larger, more
exciting slides were, or floating in an inner
tube along the Sometimes Raging Rapids
where I had the option of taking a detour
that carried me over a series of waterfalls.
But I also really liked getting a weekly pay-
check because I had an addiction to buying
clothes. As far as I was concerned, a girl
could never have enough outfits.

The waves began to diminish. The
buildup was slow, the letdown a little faster.
I really wanted to just dive into the pool. It
was nearing the end of June and was hot.

"Hey!"

I glanced down. Romeo was looking up
at me, water dripping from his hair. His hair
touched his shoulders. I wondered if it curled
when it was dry. The water was lapping at
his chest, and since I sat at the five-foot
marker, I figured he was tall. Jock tall. I no
longer liked jocks.

"Can I put her on my shoulders now?" he
asked, like someone who smells chocolate

chip cookies baking and is asking for permission to snitch one. In other words, he knew the answer was no but he asked anyway.

"No." Okay, I have to admit that having power gave me a rush. Not that I ever abused it.

"Why not?"

"Too dangerous."

What was he doing hanging around here anyway? Why wasn't he playing at Surf's Up where he could do some actual surfing on a man-made surfing machine? I wanted to think it was because he didn't have the skills, but the truth was he looked as though he had skills in a lot of areas. Obviously I was influenced by a nice tan much more than I should have been.

"What's your name?" he called up.

I shook my head. We weren't supposed to flirt with guests. We were supposed to be seriously watching the swimmers. Not that I hadn't done my share of flirting with

Tanner. Or it had felt like flirting at the time. I was pretty new at it so maybe I hadn't been as clever and flirtatious as I thought. Maybe I'd just been stupid. I hadn't been able to hold on to him.

"Hey, come on," Romeo said. "What's the big deal?"

I once again pointed to the sign. "Number ten."

NO TALKING TO THE LIFEGUARDS.

I'd been offended when I'd first read the sign. It reminded me of signs that they posted at the zoo warning people not to feed the animals.

For some reason Romeo laughed, and I wondered if he was thinking the same thing about the sign that I was. He had a terrific laugh. Deep, infectious. It made me want to laugh with him. It almost made me want to give him my name.

Trying to appear bored, I looked across the pool but I still could see him out of the corner of my eye.

Then he swam away.

I didn't want to admit that I was a little disappointed that he gave up so easily. On the other hand, now that he was swimming in the pool, he became someone who I was *supposed* to watch.

Sometimes work was no fun at all.

CHAPTER THREE

A couple of hours later, I was stretched out on a lounge chair on the Tsunami deck, eyes closed, soaking up the sun, waiting for Robyn and Whitney to catch up with me for lunch. Since this was my work area, I was always the first one to arrive. I suppose it would have been fairer to switch around where we ate, but the truth was that my area had the best views of guys.

Originally I'd been thrilled about that aspect, but after my experience with Tanner, I was no longer sure that I wanted a summer romance. As a matter of fact, I was pretty sure I didn't. I just wanted to work, shop, hang out with friends. Maybe later, I'd take a more serious interest in guys again, maybe when school started —

"Hey, if it isn't the rules girl stretched out on my lounge chair."

I heard another lounge chair scrape over the ground as someone sat on it. Droplets of water slapped my bare arm. I'd taken off my sunglasses because I didn't want big white ovals of non-tanned skin around my eyes, so I had to squint to see who had disturbed me. Although I thought I'd recognized the voice. It just sounded a little different close up, when it wasn't being yelled across water.

Romeo.

His wet hair fell across his brow again, and he did a little flick of his head to get it out of the way. More droplets slapped my arm. It appeared that keeping his hair out of his eyes was a constant battle, because almost immediately the heavy locks fell back over his forehead. His sunglasses prevented me from telling the exact color of his eyes.

When he was in the pool and not wearing shades, I could tell that they were a light color. Blue maybe. Like the sky at noon. Not that I really cared about his rebellious hair or the color of his eyes. I just wanted him to go away.

"I don't think it's yours. No towel, no bag, no item showing that you claimed this spot," I told him with authority. After all, I still had my whistle, which meant I was the girl in charge.

"Right there. My Birks."

I leaned over and looked beneath the chair, where he was pointing. No way those were there when I sat down.

I grabbed my sunglasses from where they rested beside my hip and put them on. It's easier to be intimidating when you're not squinting. "Sorry, but it doesn't count when you slip them under there *after* someone has sat down."

"Why would I do that?"

"To irritate me, because I wouldn't let you swim with Juliet on your shoulders."

"Juliet?" Then, as though a lightbulb had gone off, he grinned broadly. "That's good. Clever even. So you caught that my name is Romeo, huh?"

"Hard to miss when your girlfriend is screaming it at the top of her lungs."

"She's not my girlfriend."

Okay, this was too much like my experience with Tanner earlier in the summer. No-commitment Tanner, as I'd started to think of him. Too-many-girls-too-little-time Tanner. I thought of a new name for him almost every day. I knew I needed to get over what had happened, but what can I say? I was crushed.

"Does she know that?" I asked.

"I hope so. She seemed pretty smart."

I just bet. "Could you go away, because I'm trying to take a break here?"

"So what's your name?" he asked as though I hadn't spoken, as though I wasn't trying to get him to run off and play with some other girl.

"Good-bye."

"Bummer! You've got cruel parents. What were they thinking to name you that?"

I had to fight really hard not to smile at his teasing. And talk about cruel parents. *Romeo?* But I wasn't mean enough to point that out. No reason to make him feel badly about his name just because I wanted him to leave.

Why was he even over here? I wasn't going to tease back. I wasn't going to indicate that I had any interest at all. I had a new rule: only one heartbreak per summer. I'd reached my limit.

"I bet it gets really hard when you're at a party and everyone starts leaving," he said as though he wasn't at all bothered by my ignoring him. "I mean, you have to wonder — are they really saying good-bye or do they want to talk to *you*?"

Groaning, I shook my head and closed my eyes. I wasn't going to be influenced by his cuteness or the fact that he seemed as though he might be a lot of fun. Been there, done that.

I felt a disturbance near my hip-pack — where I'd clipped my park ID earlier. My eyes sprung open in time to see him holding my ID and reading my name.

"Caitlin. I like it," he said.

"Like I care what you like," I said, shooing his hand — as though it was a pesky mosquito — away from my badge.

"So why are you giving me such a hard time?" he asked.

"You're a player. Obviously."

"Why? Because people call me Romeo?"

"You're here with another girl. Shouldn't you pay attention to her?"

"Actually, I'm *not* here with another girl. I just met her this morning. We were hanging out in the pool for a while. She's off doing something else now."

Why was he telling me all this? Didn't my attitude say "I don't care"? And where were Robyn and Whitney? I sat up, looked around, and spotted them at a nearby table. Robyn wiggled her fingers at me. Great. We were supposed to be lifeguards, rescuing people. Why couldn't she and Whitney see that *I* needed rescuing?

"Gotta go," I said. "My lunch partners are here."

I picked up my soft-sided cooler.

"Later," he said.

I didn't want to be totally rude so I gave him a halfhearted wave. I crossed over the sand that made this part of the park look like an island. I dropped into the chair at the table. "Thanks, y'all, for coming to my rescue."

"I didn't realize you wanted rescuing," Robyn said.

"Well, I did."

"Who's the cutie?" Whitney asked.

"Romeo," I stated flatly.

Robyn laughed. "No way!"

"Yeah. That's what I thought. I've already had one Romeo this summer, thanks so very much."

"I hate when people make judgments

about someone without really knowing the person or make a decision based on someone else," Whitney said.

"What are you talking about?" I asked, opening my cooler and taking out my sandwich.

"Just because Tanner turned out to be a jerk doesn't mean this guy is."

"For most of the morning he was in the pool with another girl, then he comes over and starts talking to me. *Hello?!* That tells me all I need to know."

"You're harsh."

This from Miss I'm-So-Adorable-No-One-Ever-Says-No-to-Me. Don't get me wrong. I liked Whitney but somehow she always, and I mean *always*, got what she wanted. Worked where she wanted, when she wanted, with as much or as little effort as she wanted. And if she wanted the park owners to throw a party for the employees? They did. The employee get-together where Tanner had decided he wanted to kiss someone else had been Whitney's idea.

She liked parties. So did I. But it was as though she had some secret password or something. And she wouldn't share it.

Robyn had been my best friend forever. I knew everything about her. Well, almost everything. It had been a shock to learn that she liked my brother.

But we'd only known Whitney for a few weeks. We were still trying to figure her out. No matter how much time we spent together, no matter how much she talked, she never really told us anything important. It was as if she didn't really want us to know anything about her except for surface stuff. She never shared deep, dark secrets.

"So . . . you don't have a boyfriend," I said. "Go say hi to Romeo if you think he's not going to break your heart."

"Maybe I will."

I issued another challenge with a look over the top of my sunglasses.

"Fine. Okay. I will." She got up and walked away.

I glanced over my shoulder. Romeo was

stretched out on the lounge chair that I'd been sitting on. Had his Birks been under the chair when I got there and I just missed them? And what was so special about that chair anyway? A lot of empty ones were available.

Whitney sat down on the lounge chair beside Romeo and started talking to him. He sat up and grinned at her. Of course, here was another girl to flirt with. I knew I shouldn't be disappointed by how quickly he took an interest in her. But I was. Sometimes I felt like such a mess.

"That girl takes bold to a whole new level," I said.

"I know what you mean. Sometimes, I don't think she's afraid of anything."

"Except for media coverage."

When Robyn had saved the kid from drowning, Whitney had been with her, but afterward she'd disappeared into the background like Spider-Man or something — not wanting any credit, not wanting to be interviewed. Robyn had been on the news that night, talking about what she'd done. She'd been great at it. She'd always been shy, but she'd sort of come into her own with the whole rescue incident.

Or at least that's how my mom described it when she watched the news coverage.

I was trying really hard not to pay any attention to the exchange between Romeo and Whitney. He said something. She laughed. He grinned. Even from here, his grin had power, made my stomach flutter. He gave off vibes as though he was all about having fun, maybe being a little bad.

But this was girl number three — that I knew about — and the park had only been open a little more than three hours. He was a major flirt.

"Whitney really seems to like him," Robyn said.

"Fine, she can have him." I turned my attention back to my sandwich, not to eat it, but just to wrap it up so it was ready to go into the trash. Thinking about how disastrous my summer had been so far had ruined my appetite.

I shifted my gaze to the edge of the pool where the waves rolled onto the sandy shore. Tanner was still standing there, in red swim trunks and visor, holding his rescue tube, watching the swimmers. I remembered a time when he'd watched *me*, when he would come over and talk to me during his break.

"Surprises me, though," I confessed. "I thought she liked Jake."

Jake was another summer employee. He worked the ice-cream cart, which was a total waste as far as I was concerned. His uniform was red shorts and a white polo shirt with the Paradise Falls logo on it. He was really in shape. He would have made a great lifeguard.

"She's sorta right, you know," Robyn said. "Just because Tanner was a jerk, doesn't mean this guy is or that all other guys are."

I glanced back over at Romeo. He and Whitney were having a marathon conversation. "Does he look athletic to you?"

"Definitely."

"So he's probably a jock."

"Maybe."

"And with a nickname like Romeo, he obviously has girlfriends."

"Do you think it's a nickname?" she asked.

"Would you name your kid Romeo?"

She shrugged. "I've heard worse."

"I guess. But the thing is — I'm not interested in cute jocks. I want a geek. Someone other girls don't want."

"Caitlin —"

"It hurts, Robyn, it just really hurts when you like a guy and he kisses someone else. It would have been different if Tanner hadn't let me think that he liked me. But I thought he did and then he didn't. And I don't know what I did wrong."

"You didn't do anything wrong."

I shook my head. I knew she was trying to lift my spirits, but it wasn't working. "You don't understand because you've only ever liked Sean and he hasn't hurt you yet. Of

41

course, if he does, I'll make his life miserable." I was digressing. "Anyway, I just don't want to get hurt again. And Romeo has broken hearts tattooed all over him."

"Really?" She snapped her head around to get a better look at him.

"Well, not literally," I said. "You know what I mean. You can just look at him and tell he breaks hearts."

And I wasn't going to do anything that might get my heart broken . . . ever again.

CHAPTER FOUR

Whitney was still talking to Romeo when my lunch break came to an end. I didn't want to admit how much it bothered me that they had apparently bonded. Or that I was irritated that she hadn't come back to tell Robyn and me everything she'd learned about him.

I didn't want to be interested in Romeo. I was swearing off guys.

Still, as I sat in my lifeguard chair, I kept looking back toward the sand-covered deck. Eventually I noticed that Whitney had left. The next time I looked over, I saw Romeo wading into the water. He really was in shape. His strides were long.

The waves hadn't started up yet, but I wasn't supposed to be watching cuties wading into the water. For one thing, that end of the pool wasn't my zone. For another, looking at him made my heart do this crazy dance. Distracting, very distracting.

I turned my attention back to my zone. Some people brought inner tubes into the pool and floated. Some swam. Some dove beneath the surface — those were the ones I watched most closely, waiting for them to bob back up. I even made a little game of it, trying to guess where they'd come up. Most kids couldn't hold their breath very long. But I memorized faces, did head counts, and worked really hard to make sure that everyone was accounted for.

"Your friend is nice!" Romeo called up to me.

What was it with this guy? Did he really not understand how serious my job was? That I couldn't be distracted? And why would he think that I'd care what he thought about Whitney?

I shifted my gaze back to the other people in the pool. It was always the most crowded this time of the afternoon. Not everyone got to the park right when it opened, but people who planned to come for the day were usually here by now — otherwise they really didn't get their money's worth. So the pool was packed with water-lovers.

I glanced down at Romeo. He was still there, patiently waiting for me to crack.

I did. I pointed back to the large sign.

"What if I can't read?" he called out.

"You can read."

I shifted my gaze back to my area of the pool. How could I make him go away?

The alarm sounded. People shrieked and yelled. Most of them were here because they got a thrill from the waves. We had pools without waves. Granted they weren't as large or deep, and the deck area wasn't as imaginative, but if guests didn't like waves, they did have somewhere else to go.

I found myself glancing down again. Even though I was wearing sunglasses, Romeo seemed to be able to tell when he had my attention. His grin grew. The waves were getting higher, stronger, and he was having a tough time keeping his balance.

I went back to counting the heads in my area. Out of the corner of my eye, I saw him dive into a large wave and disappear. I figured he'd surface even farther out, in another lifeguard's zone. I did a quick look around my area. Then looked to the next zone over. I didn't see Romeo surface. But that was the direction in which he'd dived.

I did a quick visual sweep of the entire pool. I didn't see him.

I stood up for a better view. The wave pool was awesome, but also dangerous. The waves went out, then came back in, just like the ocean. If a person wasn't careful, he could get caught, sucked into an undertow. With so many people floating on the surface, sometimes it was difficult to break through to the surface for air, especially if a person was at the deep end where he couldn't touch bottom.

We'd never had anyone drown in this pool, but during orientation they'd told us about people drowning at several other water parks. I told myself not to worry. Romeo was a strong swimmer. So where was he?

He couldn't hold his breath this long. I did another careful visual sweep of the pool. I breathed a sigh of relief when I saw a guy with thick, black hair — but then he turned and he wasn't Romeo.

My heart pounded. I put my whistle to my mouth, hesitated, took another look around, couldn't see him. I knew people could get tired. If they were in the deep end of the pool, they were a disaster waiting to happen.

I blew three short blasts, which was the signal for clearing the pool.

I saw the lifeguards on the towers on either side of me come to their feet and start looking around. I did three more short blasts.

They started yelling for people to get out of the pool. The lifeguards at the shallow end started ushering people out of the water. It was a little like the scene from *Jaws* when someone saw a shark. Everyone hurried to get out as though they all realized that there was danger.

"What's up, Morgan?" Trent, my supervisor, yelled at me. Trent had buzzed his brown hair. I had no idea what color his eyes were because he always wore sunglasses: outside, inside, in the dark. Always. And he called each of us by our last name as though that made us all more grown-up or something.

"I saw someone go under. He hasn't come back up."

"Are you sure?"

Was I? It was too late to have doubts. I nodded. "Absolutely."

"Okay." Using his radio, he called in for the waves to be manually shut off. When the waves are going, we can't see into the pool very well. Since the summer had started, we'd never had to shut off the waves. It was a big deal, but I just didn't see that we had a choice.

My mouth had gone dry. I didn't know if I could blow my whistle again if I had to.

There was a loud *thunk* as the wave machine was cut off before it was timed to shut down. Trent was going around to each lifeguard telling him or her to look for a drowning victim.

All the guests were out of the pool now. The waves were calming. But the pool was just so big that it was hard to get a good look. It didn't help that the sun was reflecting off the water.

"Anybody see anything?" Trent yelled.

All the lifeguards were shaking their heads.

Trent walked back over to my station. "Where'd you see him go under?"

I pointed to my zone. I climbed down from my platform. "Should we swim across the pool, search the floor? Maybe he got caught on something."

"You wouldn't happen to know his name, would you?"

He would have to ask.

"Uh, yeah, actually, I heard someone call him Romeo."

The disadvantage of working at a water park is that everyone wears sunglasses so it's really hard to know what anyone is thinking, but I noticed Trent's jaw dropped a little as though he thought maybe I was playing a prank on him.

"Romeo?" he asked. "You're not serious."

"Yeah, I'm afraid I am. Maybe it's a nickname."

He lifted his radio. "Suz, could you please announce that" — he shook his head — "that Romeo needs to report to the supervisor at the shallow end of Tsunami?"

The announcement echoed over the park. "Romeo, report immediately . . ."

It really sounded stupid. I heard a few people laugh, but most were like me: worried.

"Let's go, Morgan. If you see him, let me know."

We walked to the shallow end of the pool and I started scanning faces. "I really think we need to go into the pool," I told Trent. He walked the area, he never sat on the lifeguard platform, so I felt obligated to point out, "There are blind spots —"

"You the supervisor?" I suddenly heard.

Trent and I spun around.

Romeo stood there looking as perplexed as I felt. He wasn't wearing his sunglasses. I could see his eyes clearly. They were a pale gray, almost silver. I didn't think I'd ever seen anyone with eyes that shade before. The fact that he had intriguing eyes added to my anger.

"Where were you?" I demanded to know.

"Uh, the restroom?" He said it as though he wasn't sure. "Is that against the rules?"

"I didn't see you leave the pool."

He shrugged. "Didn't know I needed your permission."

"You don't. Sorry for the trouble," Trent said. He looked at me. "We'll talk later. Get back to your station." Blowing his whistle, he started walking through the crowd. "It's okay, folks. False alarm."

"Should I be flattered that you were worried about me or insulted that you thought I'd drown?" Romeo asked.

"Even strong swimmers drown," I grumbled before I turned on my heel and headed back to my station.

"Wow, that was some serious whistle-blowing you did," Tanner said when I walked by him.

I glared at him, but he probably couldn't tell, because I was wearing my sunglasses.

How could I have been so stupid?

"I was mortified," I told Robyn later.

When it was time for my break, I'd headed over to Mini Falls. We were sitting on the short wall that surrounded Lost Lagoon, which was a really shallow pool with a wrecked pirate ship in the middle that kids could play on. Robyn and I were dangling our feet in the water, so they were cool while the sun beat down on our backs and shoulders.

"It's better to be safe than sorry," Robyn said.

"The other lifeguards are calling me 'whistle-blower.'" They'd called me that as I walked by on my way back to my platform. It had hurt my feelings. I was usually tougher, but between Tanner and the Romeo incident, I was losing confidence in my judgment.

"They're just jealous."

"Of what? My getting the award for most panicked lifeguard of the summer?" I was the youngest lifeguard at Tsunami. I felt that I had to prove something, that I was capable of handling the job. I worked so hard to remain cool, so no one would know I had doubts.

"Caitlin, chill. If you hadn't cleared the pool and he *had* drowned, it would have been a thousand times worse."

She had a point. Still it didn't make me feel any better.

"Trent was so mad." Once he'd calmed all the guests down, he'd come over to talk to me. His voice had been low and chilling. He thought my actions reflected badly on him. He'd told me that he was going to start keeping a closer eye on me. I'd been working for a month without anyone watching me. Now, because of one instance of bad judgment, everything was suspect? It made no sense. I was starting to think the guy was psycho.

"He'd have been madder if someone had drowned," Robyn said.

I knew she was right. My job was to make sure that everyone was safe. Still, I shouldn't have even been looking at Romeo. Maybe that was what really had me upset. That I'd noticed him to begin with. If I hadn't, I wouldn't have been looking for him, wouldn't have been aware that he'd gone underwater. He'd messed up my perfect employee record by being so cute that I'd wanted to look at him.

"He said Whitney was nice."

"Who said?" Robyn asked.

"Romeo."

"When did you talk to him?"

"He keeps coming over to my area and yelling stuff up at me. If Trent saw, he would not be happy." Maybe Trent had seen him talking to me. Maybe that was the reason he'd gone postal over one little mistake.

"So maybe this Romeo guy likes you," Robyn said.

"I doubt it."

"Do you want him to?" Robyn asked.

"No." Although I guessed there was nothing wrong with a guy liking me as long as I didn't like him back. "Tanner's probably glad he dumped me."

"He didn't really dump you. You dumped him."

"His dumping me was coming. Why else would he kiss another girl?"

"Because he's an idiot."

"Maybe I'm the idiot. Maybe I should transfer to this area of the park."

"Why?"

I sighed. "Because no one around here knows me."

Robyn gave me a sympathetic smile. "You're taking this too hard. So you made a mistake. We all do. And around here, we have to watch all the little kids really carefully."

Watching carefully was what I did. I just hadn't proved it like Robyn had. Not that I wanted a reason to be a hero, because that meant bad news for someone.

I stood up. "Guess I'd better get back to work. Thanks for listening."

"That's what friends do."

"Well, you're the absolute best at it." I took a step away, turned back. "It seems like we never do anything together anymore."

"I know." She shrugged. "Between work and . . . well, you know."

Yeah, I did. Between work and my brother.

"Later," I told her.

For the first time since I started working here, I wasn't looking forward to returning to my station at Tsunami. And it was all Romeo's fault.

CHAPTER FIVE

"Look what I've got!" Whitney waved four oblong ticket-looking things in front of my face so fast that they blurred and I couldn't read them.

I was sitting on a metal bench in the locker room. It was the end of the day. Or at least the end of the park's day. Everything shut down at eight. Thank goodness. I was so ready to go home. I wasn't even sure that I'd come back tomorrow. The souvenir shop sold cheap little plastic whistles. Someone had bought a dozen and taped them all over my locker. *Ha-ha! So very funny.*

I'd pulled them off and tossed them in the trash. So I wasn't in the best of moods when Whitney came in all bubbly.

I'd changed out of my bathing suit and put on shorts and a cute purple top that had PRINCESS written across it in little fake silver gemstones. I was stuffing my bathing suit into my tote bag when Whitney's frantic waving began.

I grabbed her wrist to stop the almost-hurricane-force winds from slapping my face. "Hold on so I can read —"

She pulled free. "They're tickets to a concert for tonight. Front row. Want to go?"

Not particularly, but I didn't want to go home and mope around either. Plus Mom would ask how my day had been and I was afraid I'd start to cry. I wasn't normally one who cried over things, but it had been a crummy day. "Who's playing?" I asked.

"It's a local band that you've probably never heard of. Doesn't matter. We're going for the light show."

I laughed. "The light show? Why would I care about a light show?"

"Exactly. The fact that you don't care is the reason that we need to go."

I held up my hands to stop the madness. "Okay, start over because I'm totally lost."

She dropped onto the bench beside me. "The park is going to have a Fourth of July extravaganza, stay open late — you know that, right?"

"Sure. Sean's been talking about the different ideas they've been tossing around in marketing to promote the thing."

"Since I'm in parties and entertainment, I'm helping to plan it. Charlotte is in charge, totally, because she's the full-time permanent entertainment manager — but between you and me, she has absolutely zero imagination. Fourth of July? Fireworks. That's her amazing idea. But everyone does fireworks. I mean *everyone*. So I'm thinking laser light show. And the company that I'm thinking we might want to hire is doing a light show as part of this concert, so I want to check them out."

A couple of weeks ago, I would have told Whitney she was crazy to think that management was going to take any of her suggestions seriously. But she and Robyn had come up with the float-in movie idea, management had bought into it, and now every Thursday night, the park stayed open late and showed a movie on the white wall behind Tsunami — while guests floated in inner tubes in the pool. Like a drive-in movie, except on water.

So if Whitney wanted a laser light show instead of fireworks, I figured we'd have a laser light show.

"Going to this concert sounds like a last-minute thing," I said. "And you got *front row* tickets?"

"It's all about who you know. I called my dad. He knows people who know people. He had his assistant bring them over."

She definitely didn't live in my world. Robyn and I had gone to a concert last year and we'd only been able to afford tickets in the nosebleed section.

"So do you want to come with me?" Whitney asked.

I didn't quite trust her — which is an awful thing to say, but it was the truth. Four tickets, two girls. Was she thinking of playing Cupid? Maybe setting me up with a blind date? I liked to be in charge, Robyn liked to follow, but Whitney liked to make things happen.

"Who are the other two tickets for?" I asked.

"Robyn and Sean, of course."

Of course. I didn't particularly want to hang out with Robyn and her new boyfriend but what else did I have to do? Before this summer, I'd done everything with Robyn. I'd been happy with that — a clique of two. It had been her idea to start including Whitney in our little group, which in the end, was working out for me since Robyn now spent all her time hanging out with Sean.

"Yeah, I'm in," I said.

"Great! I'll let David know."

"Who's David?"

"The driver."

"We're going in your limo?"

Whitney's mom had died, and she had no brothers or sisters. Her dad provided a limo and driver to take her places since he worked all the time and she wasn't old enough to have a driver's license.

"Well, yeah. My dad doesn't trust anyone to drive me around except a professional driver."

"So who are you, really? A princess or something?"

She laughed — a little too loudly — like people do when they think you're too close to discovering the truth and don't want you to know it. "According to my dad." She pointed at my T-shirt. "But then, so are you. Meet us at the gate when you're ready."

"I'm ready now."

We walked out of the employee locker

room. I took out my cell phone and gave my mom a quick call to let her know what was happening. She was cool with it, especially since Sean was going to be there. She trusted him to look out for me.

I closed my phone and dropped it back into my tote bag. Looking over at Whitney, I couldn't imagine not having a mom to call. I didn't know how to tell her that or even if I should. We never really talked personal stuff, which was probably why I knew so little about her.

Then my thoughts drifted to that afternoon. I didn't know why I was interested, but I wanted to ask her what she'd been talking to Romeo about during lunch. I shouldn't be interested in him, especially after the disastrous pool-evacuation episode. But I was. Even after I'd come back from my break with Robyn, I'd been unable not to notice Romeo.

He'd spent most of the remaining afternoon in the pool alone. At one point, two younger boys who I thought were twins and looked a lot like Romeo hung out with him for a while. I wondered if maybe they were his brothers. I remembered all the times when Sean had to come to the water park with Robyn and me to watch us when we were younger. So maybe Romeo hadn't come with a girl. Maybe he had just met her, like he'd said. Which meant he worked fast, and when she wasn't around, he was looking for someone else to fill the void.

If it was Robyn walking beside me, I wouldn't have had to ask. She'd just tell me. But Whitney and I were new friends — which meant she didn't know what I was thinking. Sometimes I wasn't even sure she knew what *she* was thinking.

"So that Romeo guy," I said as though I was bored, just trying to fill in the silence between us, "you sure talked to him for a long time."

"Yeah, he was pretty interesting."

She just left it at that. I wasn't going to ask what made him interesting. I wasn't going to pry information out of her. Besides, if I asked too many questions, she might think I liked Romeo and I didn't. Not at all. With any luck, I'd never see him again.

"I heard about the pool fiasco," Whitney said.

I groaned. "Did you have to mention it?"

"I think it took a lot of guts."

Her comment surprised me. "What did?"

"To blow your whistle, evacuate the pool, create chaos."

"Thanks," I said sarcastically. "That really makes me feel better."

"No, seriously. A lot of people wouldn't have done it because they'd have been afraid of looking stupid."

"Yeah, well, I really wish I hadn't done it."

"Still, it was the right thing to do."

Her words made me feel better. I'd never really expected comfort from Whitney. Maybe we *were* becoming real friends.

We came around a corner. I saw Robyn and Sean leaning against a wall, holding hands. Reluctantly, I gave my brother credit for playing it cool with Robyn when they were at work.

"She's in," Whitney said.

"I knew she would be," Robyn said, smiling.

Sean fell into step beside me and bumped his shoulder against mine — even though he had to bend down slightly to do it.

"So what was with the emergency evacuation —"

"It was a mistake," I said before he could finish. "I was an idiot, okay?"

"I didn't mean that. It's just not like you to panic."

"I thought someone had drowned," I said curtly.

"Then you did the right thing." He put his arm around me, gave me a quick hug.

"Someone taped stupid souvenir whistles on my locker," I muttered.

"People like to tease. Don't let it get to you."

Easy enough for him to say. He wasn't the one people were teasing. Still, I did appreciate his support. We didn't usually have touchy-feely moments.

The white limo was waiting near the entrance. Robyn had ridden with Whitney several times, but I never had. I tried not to look impressed as I settled into the leather seat.

Whitney handed everyone drinks from a little refrigerator. I really didn't understand why she was working at Paradise Falls. I didn't think it was because she needed the money.

The concert was at a soccer field in a nearby town. A beverage company had built and named it after themselves. It was a new field, really nice with lots of seating. They actually used it more for concerts than soccer games. They'd covered the field with a wooden platform and set up seats so some people could be closer to the stage instead of in the stadium seating area. The concert had already begun by the time we got there. Still, we stopped at the concession stand and bought drinks and hot dogs. Then we made our way down to our seats — in the first row. Sean and Robyn went down the row ahead of us, then Whitney, then me.

The band was loud. I wasn't familiar with them, couldn't understand the lyrics, but I liked the beat of the music, moved in rhythm with it. Most of the crowd were on their feet, shouting, yelling, adding to the mayhem. There was too much noise to talk.

Whitney punched my arm and when I looked at her, she laughed and covered her ears. I guessed she was trying to tell me that it wasn't her kind of music. It wasn't mine either, but I was still glad that I'd come. It was something different. Since I was working this summer, it just seemed as though I didn't have much time to get out and really have fun.

It wasn't until near the end of the concert that the light show began. It was awesome. The lights flashed, shot up into the sky, seemed to dance in rhythm to the music. Green, yellow, orange, bright colors that sometimes shimmered, sometimes wavered.

I was totally amazed.

When the band finished playing their last song, the noise level dropped. The light show ended just as abruptly. All that sensory overload almost made me dizzy, but I loved it.

Everyone applauded, and I didn't know if they were clapping for the band or the laser light show. I was definitely clapping for the lights that had lit up the stadium.

Whitney leaned in and yelled in my ear, "Was that wicked or what?"

I gave her a thumbs-up. She was grinning from ear to ear as though she'd created the light show herself.

People stopped clapping and began leaving. I could hear them murmuring and things got even quieter.

"Can you imagine something like that — only more spectacular and in only red, white, and blue?" Whitney asked.

"More spectacular?" I asked. "I don't know how it could be."

"I bet it could be. So wouldn't this be better than fireworks?"

"It'd be great," Robyn said.

"Definitely different," Sean added.

"So do we want it?" Whitney asked.

"I think we should at least suggest it," Sean said.

"Are y'all going to be on my light show committee?" Whitney asked. "If I make this happen?"

"You bet." Sean.

"Absolutely." Robyn.

"Of course." Me.

"So what do we do now?" I asked.

"We wait," Whitney said.

People were moving around on the stage, packing things up. It seemed a little like a letdown to watch them after the show. It took away part of the magic.

"So were you impressed?" a voice — a voice I thought I recognized — asked from behind me.

I spun around. Just as I'd feared: It was Romeo. What in the world was he doing

71

here? Why did he care if I was impressed? And impressed with what exactly? I was doing that whole multiple-question-thing that I hated.

Romeo was wearing jeans and a T-shirt with the words LIGHTS FANTASTIC superimposed over glittering spotlights. He also had a baseball cap on, so he didn't have to flick his hair out of his eyes.

"We were totally impressed," Whitney said. "So who do I talk to? Your dad?"

While she'd been talking, Romeo had been looking at me as though he expected me to answer. Or maybe he was waiting to see if I'd blow my whistle at him. But I'd left it in my locker. It hadn't occurred to me until now that maybe the unfortunate incident — as I was coming to think of it — had embarrassed him as much as it had embarrassed me. At least my name wasn't shouted over the park. Should I have apologized to him for trying to save his life when it didn't need saving?

He finally shifted his attention to Whitney. "Yeah. Here's his card."

He held out a business card, and she snatched it from his grasp as though she was afraid it was going to disappear.

"Call him tomorrow," Romeo said. "We're usually booked for the Fourth by now. Well, actually, we were but, like I told you when we talked this afternoon, we had a cancellation."

This was what they'd been talking about when Whitney went over to the lounge chairs during lunch? Why hadn't she just told me that? Did everything with her have to be so mysterious?

"Tell him we want it," Whitney said.

"Okay." He grinned. I didn't like that I noticed how nice his grin was. "But don't you need to check with management or —"

"We'll take care of it and if they say no" — she shrugged — "maybe I'll throw my own party. Either way, I want a light show."

"Okay then."

"This is my team," Whitney said. "You know Caitlin already."

"Yeah, I know Caitlin." His voice got low, teasing, and I knew he was thinking about all our silly, and not so silly, encounters. Not to mention the whole false alarm thing. At least he didn't mention it. I was so tired of all the jokes about it.

"This is her brother, Sean, and Robyn. Everyone, this is Michael."

I wasn't very good at hiding my surprise. "I thought your name was Romeo," I said.

He was grinning again. "Michael Romeo, but most people just call me Romeo. I don't know why. They seem to like the name. Between you and me, it's a little embarrassing." He took a step back. "Anyway, I have to help pack up the equipment, but I'll let Dad know and we'll set up a meeting."

When he was out of earshot, I turned on Whitney, angry, hurt, and humiliated. "Why didn't you tell me that he was part of this light show idea you had?"

"Why? What difference does it make?"

"You knew I didn't like him, that's he's the reason I made a fool of myself today, clearing the pool."

"Noooo. I knew you didn't want to *talk* to him. But that doesn't necessarily translate to not liking."

Of course it did. What planet did she come from?

"And I didn't know he was behind the pool clearing."

"They called out his name —"

"So? They call out a lot of names. I don't pay attention to announcements. What's your problem anyway?" she asked.

"I don't want to work with him."

"Why not?"

Because he made my heart do these strange somersaults. It was weird. Felt funny. I didn't like it. Not one bit. This hadn't happened with Tanner. I didn't know what it meant.

"I just don't."

"Fine. Then don't be on my committee. I can find someone else."

It was strange, but her words hurt. I was expendable to everyone. Tanner. Whitney. Even Robyn, in a way.

My dad had always said it was as though Robyn and I were joined at the hip because we did everything together. And now, she was standing off to the side, holding my brother's hand.

Which left me standing alone.

CHAPTER SIX

I didn't say anything in the limo on the ride back to the Paradise Falls parking lot. I didn't say anything in the car as Sean drove Robyn home. When he pulled up in front of her house, he got out and walked her to the door.

I knew why. He wanted to kiss her good night.

I felt like such a third wheel. I moved to the front seat. I couldn't wait until I was sixteen and could drive myself around. One year to go. It was going to be the longest year of my life.

I knew I'd overreacted to the whole Romeo thing. It was kind of funny, because now that I knew his name was Michael — well, Romeo did seem to fit better. Although I didn't think I'd ever be able to call him that without thinking of lines from Shakespeare. We'd studied his works last year in English class.

And it was an interesting last name — Italian maybe. Mine was pretty boring. Morgan. Caitlin Morgan.

I wondered if Michael helped his dad with the light show. Made sense that he did. Otherwise, why was he there tonight? I wondered if Whitney liked him — in a *like*-like kind of way. It was hard to tell with her sometimes. Okay, it was hard to tell with her most of the time. True friends hung out together, shared secrets. Every now and then I did something with Whitney, but we didn't really hang out together. And we sure didn't share secrets.

How could she not know how I felt about Romeo? Did Robyn get it?

The driver's-side door suddenly opened and I jumped. Why was I so skittish?

Sean had left the car running because it was so hot outside. Not very environment friendly. Normally, I'd give him a hard time about that and we'd get into an argument since he's convinced that global warming is a myth.

"Want to talk about it?" he asked as he pulled away from the curb.

Okay, maybe an alien had taken possession of his body, because he never asked questions like that.

"It?" I asked. "Do you even know what *it* is?"

"Not really. But I know you're bummed out about something."

We only lived a couple of blocks from Robyn's. No way did I have time to go into everything that was upsetting me.

"I'm fine," I told him. I peered over at him in the darkness. It wasn't often that we actually had a dialogue. "So, what do you know about Whitney?"

"What do you mean?"

"You were the one who wanted Robyn to be friends with her. How come?"

"She just seemed like she needed a friend."

"Robyn or Whitney?"

"What kind of question is that? Robyn had you as a friend."

"*Has* me as a friend," I said as he pulled into the driveway.

He put the car in park. "That's right. *Has* you as a friend. That's not going to change just because I'm seeing her. Is that what's bothering you?"

"I don't know. Things are just different this summer. Different from past summers. Different from what I thought they'd be."

"So what's with this Michael Romeo guy?"

"You know as much as I do."

I opened the car door and got out. I wasn't going to ask my brother for advice on guys. Plus, I really didn't want to talk about Michael Romeo.

But that night after I went to sleep, I dreamed about him. We were in Tsunami and I was sitting on his shoulders. He had really nice shoulders. Then he tossed me off. I screamed his name as I hit the water.

When I swam to the surface, he was standing there. He leaned in —

And then I woke up.

My heart was hammering. Why was I even dreaming about him kissing me?

I'd thought that Tanner would kiss me — that he'd be the first. Instead he'd kissed someone else. And the problem was: I'd really wanted him to kiss me.

So I didn't want to think about Michael kissing me, because with a name like Romeo, he'd probably kiss someone else, too.

The next morning I was walking toward my lifeguard station, enjoying the peacefulness. The park hadn't opened yet. No screams or yells or laughter filled the air. It was really like being on a tropical island. Or at least what I thought being on an island would be like. I'd never actually left the mainland. Living in north Texas, we didn't have a lot of islands around us.

A slight breeze wafted around me, and the sun glinted off the water. Other employees were taking care of business or heading to their stations. Those of us who worked around water — as lifeguards or ride attendants — wore the red bathing suits. Those who took care of other aspects of the park — food vendors, kiosk clerks, souvenir-shop employees, cleanup crew — wore red shorts and white polo shirts with the Paradise Falls logo on it. We all wore red visors. And almost everyone wore sunglasses.

I loved being part of the team. Being a lifeguard was the job I had wanted most. It had been a shock to learn from Robyn that Sean had pulled some strings to get me the position I wanted. I guess I really needed to adjust my thinking where he was concerned.

Last night had been really weird — his offering to talk to me about what was bothering me. For all of my life — or at least all that I could remember — Sean and I had simply irritated each other, as though that's what brothers and sisters were supposed to do. It was strange to have him trying to be there for me.

"Hey, Caitlin!"

I swung around at the sound of Whitney's voice. She was hurrying toward me. When she caught up with me, she was a little out of breath, her blond hair swinging around her shoulders. It caught the sunlight just like the pool did.

"What's up?" I asked.

"We're having a team meeting at one o'clock so just bring your lunch to the conference room."

I released a little laugh. "Didn't you get it last night? I don't want to do this."

"Come on, Caitlin. I need you."

Shaking my head, I rolled my eyes. I didn't think Whitney needed anyone. "Yeah, right."

"Seriously. Mr. T wants the entire park to be involved — or at least representatives of each area. You represent the pools."

The park was divided into various zones: the kiddie zone where Robyn worked; the pools, which included Tsunami and the other pools throughout the park; the slides outside of the kiddie zone; and the shops, which included all the kiosks around the park.

"Whitney —"

"Come on. Robyn is representing the kiddie zone so the three of us can have some fun. Plus, we'll always be in the majority so we can push through our agenda."

I laughed. "We have an agenda?"

"I don't know. It's something I hear my dad saying sometimes before he goes into business meetings — that he has an agenda he wants to push through. Who knows what it really means? We'll just have fun and make this the best Fourth of July extravaganza ever."

"Is Romeo going to be there?"

"Romeo? Oh, you mean Michael. Yeah. The Powers-That-Be approved the light show."

I know my eyes rounded. "Already?"

"Well, yeah. They thought it was a great idea so it was easy to convince them, and the Fourth is almost here so it's not like we have time to mess around. We need to get all the details worked out quickly."

"Hey, y'all, what's going on? Secret meeting?" Robyn asked as she walked over.

"I'm trying to convince Caitlin to be part of the team."

"Oh, I thought she already was."

"Working with Michael freaks her out."

"He doesn't freak me out." Okay, he made me a little nervous, but it was only because of the way he made my heart flutter and the fact that I seemed to do stupid things when he was around. That was dangerous.

"I thought he was nice," Robyn said.

But then, she thought my brother was nice, so I wasn't sure I could trust her opinion.

"Come on, it'll be fun planning a gigantic party," Robyn continued. "Otherwise, you'll have to eat lunch alone and I know you hate doing that."

She was right. I really didn't like doing things alone. And it probably would be fun. Whitney was a little quirky. And Robyn was my BFF.

"Okay," I said, surprised that I actually sounded excited about it. Robyn and Whitney were right. It might be interesting. And it was something different, something to occupy my mind, something to think about — other than Tanner.

"Great! I'll see you later," Whitney said. She left to begin preparing for the day's birthday parties.

"She gets so excited about things," Robyn said. "I'm glad you'll be part of the team." She headed to Mini Falls, where she'd spend the morning watching little kids hurtling down slides.

I strolled over to Tsunami. Soon it would be all madness, but I had a few minutes. I sat down on a lounge chair and absorbed the peacefulness into my system. If mermaids really existed, I'd be one. I loved the water.

"Whatcha doing? Shouldn't you be working?"

I jerked at the familiar voice. Tanner. I glanced over at him. "I've got a couple of minutes."

Other lifeguards were mingling around. We had three stations along each side of the pool and two guards would stand in the shallow end. Shallow water is as dangerous as deep water.

Tanner crouched down, balancing on the balls of his feet. "So, I hear they've got big plans for the Fourth."

"Yep." I didn't think it was a secret, but I really wasn't in the mood to yammer with him either.

"You working that night?"

"Isn't everyone?"

He ducked his head, rubbed his thumb over the face of his watch. Then he looked back up at me. "I totally blew it, didn't I?"

Was he talking about with me? And why was he even over here talking to me at all?

"Totally," I said, taking some satisfaction in the fact that I sounded so like I didn't care.

"I really like you, Caitlin. Can't you have some pity for a dumb jock?"

"I don't think you're that dumb. So what happened with you and the girl from the gift shop?"

"You mean Jasmine?" He said it as if he wasn't sure that was her name.

I shrugged. "I guess. I mean, I don't know who she is. I've just seen her working in the gift shop when I walked by."

"Oh, yeah, well, her name was Jasmine."

"*Was?* It's not anymore?"

He laughed. "I'd forgotten how funny you were. Nah, I'm sure her name is still Jasmine, it's just that she and me" — he waved his hand like a magician who was about to say abracadabra and pull a rabbit out of his hat — "you know."

Actually, I didn't. Maybe he was trying to say that she and he were no more. Did it matter to me? At all? I didn't think it did. As much as I'd liked him, it seemed as though it should have mattered. Maybe I hadn't liked him as much as I thought. Or maybe Michael Romeo made me realize that other guys — interesting guys — were out there.

"Hey, Morgan, up top, let's go!"

I was startled by my supervisor's voice. Trent was in college and he had a really deep voice. And he just looked mean, probably because he always looked as though he needed to shave. I jumped up and hurried to my post. Of course, I had to pass right by him. He had his hands on his hips and he didn't look happy. I mumbled, "Sorry," as I rushed past him.

"You know better than to flirt," he said.

I swung around. "It wasn't me."

He looked at me over the top of his sun-glasses. Why do people think that makes them look intimidating? Maybe because it does.

"It wasn't," I insisted.

I was tempted to tell him to get after Tanner, but instead I just spun on my heel and hurried to my tower. I climbed up the ladder and got into position.

All I'd wanted was a few minutes of peace and instead I'd managed to get myself in trouble.

The clanging bells that sounded like buoys that rocked in the ocean announced the official opening of the park for the day. It was always madness first thing in the morning as hordes of people began rushing into the park to claim their favorite spots before getting in line for the more popular slides.

While I waited for people to reach our pool, I looked over at Tanner standing in the shallow water. He waved at me.

I felt my cheeks grow warm. I'd liked him once. I didn't know if I could let mself like him again.

CHAPTER SEVEN

I didn't want to admit it, not even to myself, but I was a little nervous about going to the meeting. Mostly because I knew that Michael Romeo was going to be there. What did we even need to discuss anyway? It was the Fourth of July so the colors would be red, white, and blue. What else did we need to decide?

I was a little suspicious. I thought maybe Whitney was making this out to be more than it should have been. I really wished that I'd arranged to meet Robyn someplace beforehand, so we could walk into the conference room together.

It wasn't like me to be shy about things. I was the bold one. She was the one who needed to be convinced to do things. So right this minute I'd be bold — even if it killed me.

I went to the employee locker room and grabbed my tote bag. My lunch was inside. I slammed my locker closed and reset the lock. Familiar routines. I was ready for this meeting. I swung around and shrieked. Robyn was standing there.

"Where did you come from?" I asked.

"*Duh?* Mini Falls." She opened her locker. "What's wrong with you anyway? You're not usually jumpy."

"Nothing's wrong. I just don't like having people sneak up on me."

"I didn't exactly sneak." She took her tote bag out of her locker. "Are you worried about Romeo?"

"What? No. I'd totally forgotten he was going to be there."

It was a good thing that I had a tiny

nose. Gave it lots of growing room when I lied.

Robyn and I walked out of the locker room together.

"Uh, Tanner talked to me this morning," I said.

She looked over at me. "Are you liking him again?"

"I don't think so."

"Good. You shouldn't."

"Don't take this wrong, but between you and me, I always thought I'd be the one who got kissed first."

"Hey, so did I. You're not shy around guys. I am. So Sean and me . . . I never expected it."

"Makes it sound like he sneaked up on you."

She grinned. "He did. I mean, really, Caitlin, he was the last guy I ever thought I'd feel this way about."

I wanted to squirm. I didn't want to know how she felt about him. "TMI."

"Whatever. I'm so glad that we let Whitney into our little circle and became friends with her, so I have someone I can talk to about Sean."

"You talk to Whitney about Sean?"

"Sure. I know you don't want to hear it, and quite honestly, I feel weird talking to you about your brother. But with Whitney, it's totally different. I can tell her how nice he is and she doesn't look at me as if I've lost my mind."

"I don't do that."

She released a short burst of laughter. "Yes, you do. I can tell her that I like him and she doesn't tell me that she doesn't get it."

"Well, I don't."

Teasingly, she shoved my shoulder. "Which is why I'm glad that I've got Whitney."

Which shouldn't have made me feel bad, but it did. I wasn't being a very good friend, but I didn't want the details about dating Sean.

We reached the offices. I was glad,

because I was having a hard time thinking of anything to say to Robyn that didn't make me sound like a horrible friend. I wasn't exactly sure how I felt about Robyn confiding in Whitney. I knew I should be glad that she had someone to talk to so she didn't have to talk to me about Sean, but we'd been best friends forever. It was strange to think of her telling someone something and not telling me.

"The conference room is at the end of the hallway," the receptionist said. She was wearing the red shorts and white polo shirt. Even the people who ran the place were dressed as though they were heading for fun in the sun. We got to the end of the hallway. Robyn opened the door.

"Oh, there you are," Whitney said. "Come on in."

One long table was in the center of the room. Whitney sat at the head of it. On her left sat Michael and Jake. Robyn sat on her right and I sat beside Robyn, so I was opposite Jake.

Michael wasn't wearing his hat so he flicked his head back to toss his curly hair out of his eyes. His eyes were still amazing to look at. I think they stood out so much because he was sitting by Jake, who had such dark brown eyes. Jake's hair was auburn, buzzed short. A lot of guys working at the park went with really short hair. It was definitely cooler, I thought, as I fluffed my fingers through mine.

"So Jake represents the vendors, Robyn represents the kiddie area, and Caitlin represents the pools. We're just waiting for someone from slides and attractions. You can go ahead and eat your lunch," Whitney said.

"Isn't everyone else eating?" I asked, noticing that no one else had any bags, sacks, or food in front of them.

"I've already eaten," Whitney said.

"Me, too," Jake and Michael said at the same time.

"Oh." I looked at Robyn. She gave her head a little shake. I agreed. I didn't want to eat in front of people who weren't eating.

Considering my recent luck, I'd probably get food caught between my teeth and no one would tell me.

The door opened. A girl walked in. She had red hair pulled back into a ponytail. "Sorry I'm late! I kept telling my supervisor that I had to go but he wouldn't listen. Sometimes I think he doesn't quite trust me. I don't understand why not."

I did. She was totally untrustworthy. I tried not to stare, but I couldn't seem to help myself. She was the last person I expected, or wanted, to see.

She plopped into the chair beside me. "Hey, guys, I'm Jasmine. I'm so psyched about being on this committee. Plus, it gets me away from all the insanity."

"I thought you worked in the gift shop," I said.

"I did. But I moved to slides. And I'm loving it, but it's just madness."

She didn't look at me while she talked. She gazed at Michael. She smiled at him. He grinned at her.

Déjà vu.

"Okay, everyone, I'm sorta in charge," Whitney said. "Charlotte is the manager of events" — she made quote marks in the air — "so she'll have final say. But we do the brainstorming and then I tell her what we're planning. We're going to come up with ideas for the Fourth that will knock off socks — or, I guess in our case, flip-flops."

Michael grinned at Whitney. He really did have a cute grin. I wondered if he liked her. They'd obviously connected yesterday during lunch and had seemed comfortable around each other last night. And she hadn't done anything to embarrass him, like cause his name to be shouted over the park's intercom system.

Jake was leaning back in his chair, as though he had as much interest in this meeting as I did, which amounted to zero interest. But he was watching Whitney. I wondered why he didn't hang out with her. I was pretty sure that he liked her. He seemed to be with her when it was convenient, but he never went out of his way to be with her. Or at least that was my take on it. Still, I had the feeling that there were things going on —

"Okay, Caitlin?"

Whitney using my name brought me back to the mission. I glanced around the table.

Jasmine raised her hand. "I'll do it."

"No, I'll do it," I insisted, not even knowing what it was I was agreeing to do. I didn't even realize that I'd been asked to do something. Jasmine had taken away my crush. I wasn't going to let her take this, too. Whatever it was.

"Great," Michael said and stood up.

Not so great.

Robyn leaned over and whispered, "You're going to show him around the park."

"Why? He was here yesterday. He knows what the park looks like." I hadn't lowered my voice. I didn't see the point.

"But yesterday I was looking at it differently," Michael said. "Yesterday was all about fun. Now it's all about work."

Jasmine laid her head on the table and stretched her body across the polished wood like someone in a yoga class reaching out. "I'll *doooo* it."

If it was anyone else asking, I would have said, "Go ahead." I really didn't feel comfortable being alone with Michael — but only because of the whole making-a-fool-of-both-of-us thing at the park yesterday. I might have to work up the courage to apologize. But Jasmine had stolen one boy from me and I wasn't about to let her steal another. Not that Michael was with me, but still. Jasmine was not to be trusted. I stood up. "I've got it."

I sounded way more confident about doing this than I felt.

"Fantastic," Whitney said. "While you're gone, we'll brainstorm the songs that will play with the light show." She looked at Michael. "Any restrictions?"

"None. Whatever you want us to play we'll play and coordinate the lights to match. That's what we do."

I forced myself to pick up my tote bag and follow Michael out of the office. Once we got outside, we both slid on sunglasses. I released the breath I hadn't realized I'd been holding. "Look, about yesterday —"

"Forget about it. You were right to make sure that I wasn't in trouble in the pool. I'm cool with it."

"Wish my supervisor felt that way."

"What? He thought you were wrong?"

"I think he's a little embarrassed."

"Tell him to get over it."

"Obviously, you've never had a supervisor. You don't exactly talk back to him, not if you want to keep your job."

"Other than yesterday's fiasco, do you like working here?" he asked.

"Love it." I glanced around, a little more comfortable with him, but not wanting to like him any more than I already did. "You know, I could probably get you a map of the park and you could just do this on your own."

"Wouldn't be as much fun."

"And you like to have fun."

"I'm all about the fun."

"So why do you need to see the park?" I asked.

"Trying to figure out where we want to set up the light show. I'm thinking by the wave pool is best, so let's start there."

We started walking toward Tsunami.

He ran his hand through his hair, pushing it back instead of flicking his head. "I've never actually arranged a light show before. Dad will come in and check out all my decisions. But he said I could do the preliminary."

"So this is what? A hobby or something?"

"Nope. It's his business. Lights Fantastic."

We got to Tsunami, and Michael stopped. He slowly turned around. "Yeah, this is probably the best place."

"Thought you wanted a tour."

He grinned. "Nah. I'm just not into meet-ings. All we need to know is where we're going to set up and the songs you want. For the Fourth, I figure patriotic."

He really seemed like a nice guy. I wish he didn't. *I know. I know.* Who doesn't want a guy to be nice? But it was kind of scary to even think about liking a guy again.

Then it started to get awkward because neither of us was saying anything.

"At Christmas, my dad set the lights on our house to blink in time to music," I said. "It was neat."

"My dad does that, too. Actually, part of his business is doing it for other people. Gets crazy right after Thanksgiving."

"Do you help with those lights, too?"

"Oh, yeah. We create a simulation on the computer first to figure out how we need to set up everything."

"So you're a geek?"

"Big-time." He grinned, obviously not bothered by the word. "What did you think of the light show last night?"

"Cool. Totally," I told him.

Then we were quiet again.

"Why don't you go ahead and eat?" he asked. "We can sit right over there."

At the end of the sandy deck were two empty lounge chairs, with no Birks beneath them.

"I don't know," I began. "I'd feel funny —"

"You don't want to pass out from starvation."

"I'm hardly starving."

Without waiting, he sat on a lounge chair. Then he grinned. "Come on. I don't bite."

He was so cute, and it was so tempting . . . but the fact that it was tempting was the reason that I didn't want to do it.

"If you're finished looking around, we should probably go back to the meeting," I told him.

"Do you really want to sit in a meeting?" He made an arc with his hand as though he was drawing a rainbow in the air. "It's such a nice day."

It was a nice day. It was a shame to waste it in an office. I sat on the chair beside his. I was hungry. I opened my bag. "Want some chips?"

"No. I really did eat before I headed over here. My mom fixed a big pot of spaghetti."

"Is your family Italian?" I asked before I bit into my sandwich.

"You bet. Small family though. There's Mom and Pop. And my twin brothers. How about you?"

I almost choked on my sandwich. "How about me what?"

"How about your family? I met your brother last night. Is he it?"

"Yeah. Besides Mom and Dad."

"Must be fun to work here."

"You'd think."

"It isn't?"

I popped a chip into my mouth, offered him the opened bag. He broke down and took one.

"It's not that it isn't fun," I told him, "but it's not as much fun as visiting."

But I didn't really want to talk about me.

"So how will you do the light show?" I asked.

"Probably set things up on both sides of the pool. Use the park's announcement system to play the music. I know firsthand that it works really well and can be heard all over the park."

I groaned. "Look, I'm really sorry about that."

He grinned. "I'm just teasing you. It made me feel important, hearing my name."

"Yeah, right."

"Seriously. My first thought was that one of my brothers had gotten into trouble, so I was glad it was nothing."

"I'm not sure I'd classify it as nothing. We did clear the pool. I couldn't believe I hadn't seen you leave."

"So you were watching for me?"

I was really saying more than I wanted to say. "Not really. Maybe that's the reason I missed seeing you."

He took another chip. "Maybe."

"So why do you need the music to be heard all over the park?"

"Because people will be able to see some of the lights no matter where they are in the park. The best seats will be around here, of course. I think it'll be cool."

I thought it would be, too. I looked at my watch. I didn't want Trent yelling at me again. I was running out of time.

"I'm going to have to go," I said as I wadded up the empty chip sack.

"Already?"

"Yeah, we only get half an hour for lunch."

I stood up and slung my tote bag over my shoulder. He stood up, too.

"Can I ask you a question?" I asked.

"Sure."

"The Birks beneath the lounge chair yesterday — were they there when I sat down?"

"Probably."

I arched an eyebrow. "Probably?"

"They weren't mine."

My jaw dropped. "What?"

"Hey." He held up his hands. "In all fairness, I thought they were, but when I went to put them on, they were too big. I felt pretty stupid."

I couldn't help myself. I laughed. "I can't believe you did that!" Or that he was so comfortable admitting it to me. Nothing seemed to phase him.

"Michael!"

I snapped my head around. The two boys I'd seen with Michael yesterday slammed into him, giggling and laughing as though they wanted to tackle him.

"No running," I said, automatically shifting into lifeguard mode.

Michael laughed. Both boys stuck their tongues out at me. They looked alike. I'd seen twins before, of course, but it was still a little unsettling to see two boys who were a perfect match.

"Hey, Tony, Tommy," Michael chastised. "She's right, dudes, so don't do that."

Michael shifted his attention to me. "These are my brothers."

"They look like you. Sorta." They had the same dark hair and light silver eyes. "Not as much as they look like each other though."

"What's your name?" one of the boys asked.

"Caitlin." I wanted to reach out and ruffle his hair. It was something I did when I babysat kids and thought they were cute.

The twins looked at each other and then each gave me a mischievous grin. They started singing in unison, "Michael and Caitlin sitting in a tree —"

I felt my cheeks grow warm.

"Hey, dudes," Michael scolded, trying to put his hands over their mouths.

They roared out their laughter and ran off.

"No running!" I yelled after them.

Michael looked back at me. "Sorry 'bout that. Kids. What are you gonna do?"

"Yeah. Really. Listen, I've got to get back to work."

"Sure. Thanks for helping me pick the place to set up."

I scoffed. "I didn't do anything." I gave him a little wave. "See ya."

I had all of two minutes to get my tote bag to my locker and get back to my station. I was going to be late. I thought about asking Whitney for a tardy slip, but that seemed so juvenile. As I passed back by the offices, the light-show team was coming out the door. Jake walked on, probably because he was going to be late to work as well, and ice cream was waiting to be scooped.

Whitney, Robyn, and Jasmine caught up with me. I guess we were all headed to the employee locker rooms.

"So what did he decide?" Whitney asked.

"Tsunami."

"I figured."

"He is so dreamy," Jasmine said.

"I thought you were with Tanner," I told her.

"Nope."

She quickened her pace, going ahead of us.

"Why did you ask her to be on the team?" I asked Whitney.

"I didn't. I didn't know anyone working at slides so I asked them to just send someone. What's the problem?"

"She's the one who was kissing Tanner."

"Oh, right. I'd forgotten. She's not memorable."

"She's red-haired and way too bubbly. How can she not be memorable?" I asked.

"Sorry. I didn't remember her. I guess I could replace her."

"No, don't do that," I said. "I'm not totally mean."

"You're not mean at all," Robyn said. "Wonder why she moved to slides."

"I heard she had a problem counting change," Whitney said.

"You sure do hear a lot," I muttered.

"Hey, I work in the offices now. It's gossip central."

"Yeah, like what else have you heard?"

"Nothing I can repeat at this time. Later," she said. "I'm going to talk to Charlotte about some of our ideas."

She headed back to the offices. I looked at Robyn. "Does she not understand the friend code? That there's a dome of silence around you, so you can tell your friends things that you aren't supposed to and they won't tell anyone else?"

"Do you tell her secrets?"

"No."

"There you go."

I didn't like it when Robyn was so practical.

"I thought Michael was nice," she said.

"Based on what?" I asked as I started walking back to the lockers. I really was going to need that tardy slip.

"Well, he looked nice. He has a nice smile. And his eyes. My gosh. I've never seen eyes like that. What are they? Gray?"

"More like silver," I said.

"Is that what they put on his driver's license?"

"I don't know." I didn't even know if he had a driver's license. How old was he anyway?

"I asked them to put chocolate on my restricted license, but they didn't," Robyn said.

I laughed. I hadn't known that. Amazing what I was discovering that I didn't know about Robyn. "Why would you do that?"

"Because brown sounded so boring. And you have such pretty blue eyes."

What can I say? I do.

"So what do you think of this Fourth of July extravaganza?" Robyn asked.

"It seems pretty straightforward. I don't know why we need a committee."

"Because Whitney wants one."

"But *why*?" I asked. "Michael didn't really need a tour of the park. We walked to Tsunami and that was it. Decision made."

Robyn looked around like someone who was about to do something she shouldn't do and was afraid of getting caught. "I don't think she has any friends."

"You mean money can't buy friendship?"

Robyn gave me a look that said she was a little tired of my attitude where Whitney was concerned. "We don't know that she's rich."

I blinked in astonishment. "Of course she is. She has a chauffeur."

"Okay. So she probably is. But like I said, I don't think she has anyone to hang out with so she looks for reasons to do things that require other people."

"Sad." Really, I thought it was. Then an awful thought struck me. "Day after tomorrow? Day off? Is she hanging out with us?"

"Would you mind?"

Okay, what was I supposed to say to that? Sean had to work that day. Robyn and I were off. We hadn't had any real time together since she started hanging out with my brother. No more spending time in my room gossiping. No more hanging out at the mall. Of course, the mall thing could be because we were working so we didn't have a lot of time to shop.

But if I said I didn't want Whitney to hang out with us, I'd look selfish wanting Robyn all to myself. And it wasn't that. I just wanted to talk about how confused I was about guys all of a sudden. Why was Tanner talking to me again? Should I be interested in Michael? Or was he really a Romeo? More of a Romeo than Tanner anyway.

"I don't mind." I tried to sound bubbly, but bubbly had never been my thing.

"Are you sure?"

"Yeah, I'm sure."

"Great. We're going to have fun."

"What are we doing?"

"I don't know yet. But we'll have a great time whatever we decide."

That was the thing about Robyn. Since she'd started dating my brother, she was the eternal optimist.

While I started my day at the five-foot station, every twenty minutes we rotated. So I moved down to the station at the three-foot end of the pool, then I did a turn standing in the shallow end before moving to the station at the eight-foot mark. Then I'd take a break and start all over again. My side was the right side of the pool. Those doing the left side of the pool did the same sort of rotation. It was supposed to keep us alert. Because really and truly, watching other people having fun is boring.

That afternoon I was having a particularly difficult time staying alert. I was standing in the shallow end of the pool — which put me close to the sand-covered lounging deck. And sitting in a chair on the front row was Romeo.

He hadn't gone home after our meeting. I guess he figured since he was here, he might as well play. His brothers showed up every now and then. So Romeo was probably babysitting.

And watching me. I could feel him watching me — even though my back was to him. I had a strong urge to spin around, blow my whistle, and tell him to cut it out. But that would make me look like a psycho because I couldn't prove he was watching me.

The horn blew to warn that the waves were starting up. A lot of the smaller kids screeched and ran out of the pool, splashing water on me as they went by. I didn't mind getting splashed. As a matter of fact, it felt pretty good.

I became aware of a shadow easing up beside mine in the rippling water. I cut my eyes to the side. Romeo. No surprise there.

"You ever get a day off so you can have fun?" he asked.

"We're not supposed to talk," I said.

"You were talking yesterday."

I gave him an incredulous look. "Not while I was on duty."

"Sure you did. When you told me that I couldn't put Juliet on my shoulders."

"I can yell at people. Don't make me yell at you." Just before I turned my attention back to the swimmers, I caught a glimpse of his grin. He had *such* a cute grin.

"Romeo! Hey!"

That got my attention. I looked over my shoulder. It was Jasmine. She was holding a large cup of ice cream.

"I'm on break. I brought you some ice cream," she said.

He looked surprised. "You brought that for me?"

"I thought we could share. Come on."

"Since she can talk and you can't . . ." he said, his voice trailing off as he headed back to his lounge chair.

Since she was on break and I wasn't . . .

Not that it mattered. I wasn't going to flirt with him. He was kind of like a bee, flying from flower to flower. Only for him, the flower was whatever girl was available. He wasn't a Michael. He really was a Romeo.

And Jasmine. How had she even known that Michael was still here? Did she have some sort of guy radar? And what was it with her going after guys who talked to me?

I didn't think I knew her from school. Maybe she got bored easily. Maybe that was the real reason that she went from the souvenir shop to slides. I didn't want to think about her feeding ice cream to Romeo. But when I glanced over my shoulder, I saw that she was doing exactly that. Then giggling as though she'd just told him a joke.

"Morgan, what are you doing?"

I jerked my head around. Trent was standing there, with his hands on his hips. I'd been a perfect employee for almost a month. And because of one little incident yesterday, he'd lost all faith in my abilities. It was annoying and I didn't know how to regain his trust.

With his first two fingers, he pointed at his eyes, then he pointed out toward the pool. "That's where you're supposed to be looking."

I swallowed hard. "I know."

"Then do it."

"I am."

"Looking away, you miss seeing things."

I knew what he was thinking. "I didn't look away yesterday."

Shaking his head, he walked away. I was mortified. I really, really hoped that Romeo didn't see me getting into trouble. I wanted to look over my shoulder to see if he'd noticed. But I forced myself to keep my eyes on the swimmers.

I concentrated on the whistling breeze going over the roaring waves. The screams and laughter of the swimmers. The shrieks as kids threw sand at one another. When I did all that, I didn't hear Jasmine's light laughter or Romeo's deep chuckle.

I wasn't like Jasmine. When I laughed, people heard me. My mom said I had a joyful laugh, and I didn't laugh loudly on purpose, it's just that when I thought something was funny, I laughed first and then thought about what I sounded like later. I really hated that having Jasmine near was making me look at myself critically. So what if Tanner had kissed her instead of me? So what if Romeo was sharing ice cream with her?

So what? So what? So what?

I spun around and blew my whistle as loud as I could. Jasmine shrieked and jerked her arms and legs like a puppet that had all the wrong strings pulled. She dropped the cup of ice cream in the sand — upside down.

I almost burst out laughing, but that would be so uncool.

"Sorry," I said. "I saw kids running."

"Well, duh, it's a play area," Jasmine said.

"But they aren't supposed to run. They could trip and hurt themselves. We could get sued. It's my responsibility to protect the swimmers, the guests, and the park."

"And it is rule number one," Romeo said as though he was conspiring with me. "I don't understand how people cannot see that big board with all the rules."

"Kids can't read," Jasmine said.

"Which is why I have to blow my whistle."

"Whatever. You made me drop my ice cream. You owe me."

I owed her? Yeah, I did but not for the ice cream.

I tapped my watch. "Shouldn't you be back at your post?"

She stood up, patted Romeo on the shoulder, then leaned down and whispered something in his ear that made him grin.

I watched her start to walk away and turned my attention back to the pool. The waves were starting to die down. Pretty soon it'd be calm water again. Or as calm as it can be with a hundred and fifty people jumping around in it.

"So what was up with the whistling?" Romeo asked as he came to stand beside me.

"Like I said. Saw kids running around."

He walked past me into the water, then turned around so he was walking backward into the pool, facing me. "What's your favorite song?"

I shrugged.

"Come on. You've gotta have a favorite song."

"'Our Song' by Taylor Swift. What's yours?"

"Not important." He turned and dove into the water.

I wondered if he'd be here tomorrow and the day after that. I wondered if it would be weird to spend my day off at the place where I worked.

Probably.

Still, it was worth thinking about.

CHAPTER EIGHT

Before we'd left Paradise Falls the night before, Whitney had told her committee members that we'd have another meeting the next day and food would be provided. Sounded good to me. I didn't have to mess with fixing my lunch.

What she didn't say was that it was an experimental meal. It was based on the reason behind our committee. The Fourth of July. Red, white, and blue.

I could live with the red, white, and blue cotton candy. I didn't mind the patriotic popcorn. I thought it was neat actually, with each fluffy piece being red, white, or blue.

But I drew the line at white buns with red ketchup and blue hot dogs. I didn't want to think about the amount of dye that must have been injected into the hot dog to turn it blue.

Whitney's committee members were sitting around the table in the conference room, staring at their "provided lunch" on plates in front of them as though they thought the hot dogs would bite. Michael wasn't there. Our food selection didn't have anything to do with the light show. I was wishing I wasn't there either.

"Come on," Whitney said. "Try it."

I noticed that she wasn't chomping down on hers. "You try it," I said.

"I'm a vegetarian."

I laughed. "Since when?"

"Since I was twelve."

I tried to remember if I'd ever seen her eat any meat. Couldn't remember ever seeing her eat *anything*, actually.

"I think I'll barf if I try to eat it," Jasmine said.

I never expected to agree with Jasmine, the guy-stealer. Because she had red hair, she had a lot of freckles but they were small and disgustingly cute. Guys probably liked them. She was slender. She could probably eat sweets on non-holidays.

"Don't you think it'll be awesome for the park to serve patriotic food on the Fourth?" Whitney glanced around the table, her deep green eyes imploring someone to make the sacrifice for her.

"All right. I'll give it a try," Jake finally said.

Why was I not surprised? I thought maybe he was crushing on Whitney, but was trying really hard not to let anyone know. He seemed shy, which I so didn't get because he was really cute. And watching the way Whitney studied him, I thought maybe she thought so, too. Or maybe she was craving the hot dog. I couldn't imagine never eating meat.

Jake took a bite, chewed, swallowed,

nodded. "Not bad. Tastes like a hot dog." He finished eating it in three bites.

"I'll take your word for it," I said, shoving my plate to the center of the table.

"You lack an adventuresome spirit," Jasmine said, winking at Jake before taking a bite of her hot dog. The girl was fickle.

"What are you — a fortune cookie?" I asked.

Robyn kicked me underneath the table. It was a not-so-subtle reminder that I didn't always play well with others and that I was edging toward one of those moments. Who could blame me? I'd wanted to play with Tanner, and Jasmine had convinced him to play with her instead. And yesterday with Michael —

"So why isn't Romeo here?" Jasmine asked.

She was back to Romeo after having her moment with Jake? She was really too much.

"He'll be at tomorrow night's meeting," Whitney said, but her voice was a little tight, as though maybe she was thinking Jasmine needed to be off the team. Fine with me.

"What meeting tomorrow night?" I asked.

"We're having a team meeting tomorrow night after the park closes. Did I forget to mention that? Lights Fantastic is going to set up a couple of lights to get some readings and measurements or something. I figured we should be there."

"Most definitely," Jasmine said. "I could file a report if no one else wants to be there tomorrow night."

Not to be mean, but I didn't think she knew how to file anything except a fingernail.

"Thanks, Jasmine, but I really want the entire team there," Whitney said.

"Whatever."

"Well, yeah, since I'm the person in charge."

I had a feeling that Whitney liked Jasmine about as much as I did. Imagine that. We were in sync. By the end of summer, maybe we'd be best friends.

"Why are you in charge?" Jasmine asked.

"Because it was my idea."

"You thought of the Fourth of July?"

Jake's mouth dropped open. Me? I figured Jasmine's dumbness was just an act. Maybe she thought guys dug stupid girls. But I knew my brother didn't, and I figured he was pretty typical for a guy.

I stood up. "I'm outta here. I gotta get something to eat — something that's a normal color — before I go back to work."

Everyone else mumbled something about needing to eat, and Whitney adjourned the meeting.

"She's a piece of work," I said to Robyn as we headed to the food court. Without me saying it, she knew who I was talking about: Jasmine.

"Don't let her bug you."

"She was hanging all over Michael yesterday."

"So, do you like him?"

"No."

"Then why do you care?"

"It's just not fair that she can get any guy's attention."

"She might get it but she can't hold it. She and Tanner already broke up."

"If they were really even together for more than a kiss."

We went to Scavenger's. Although it was a sturdy building, it looked like a shack that would collapse at any moment, as though it had survived a storm. It was all part of the island illusion. They served hot dogs, nachos, popcorn, candy, and anything else unhealthy. Robyn and I each bought a regular-colored hot dog. We sat at a table beneath an umbrella.

"So *does* Whitney like Jake?" I asked.

"I think so. They sorta hang around together, but he hasn't really asked her to do anything with him. She always does the asking."

"She tells you everything, doesn't she?"

"No, not really."

"What do you think her big secret is?"

"I don't know. I think Sean knows. I'm trying not to get mad at him for not telling me."

"He knows if he told you that you'd tell me. I mean, best friends tell each other everything and he knows it."

A little secretive smile spread over her face before she bit into her hot dog.

Okay, she wasn't telling me some things, but that was okay. Because I knew I didn't really want to know if it involved my brother.

After we finished eating, we headed in opposite directions. She went back to Mini Falls and I strolled to Tsunami. The wind picked up and I could see dark clouds rolling in. I groaned. It was always a pain when it rained. Well, not the rain so much. The lightning. If we spotted lightning or heard thunder, we had to clear the pools. I'd had more than enough of evacuating pools this week.

As I neared Tsunami, I started glancing around. I didn't even realize what I was looking for until I spotted Michael and my heart gave a little kick. He was playing in the water with his brothers. He hadn't arrived before I left for the meeting, so I'd figured he wasn't coming today. I'd been disappointed. But now I felt this strange little excitement.

I watched as he picked up one of his brothers and started to swing him around —

Michael came to an abrupt stop. I didn't know if it was because he saw me and thought I'd blow my whistle at him or if he was just glad to see me.

"Morgan, you're dawdling. People are waiting to eat."

Trent. Why was it that lately he was always catching me at the worst possible moment? I hurried to my station and relieved the guy who was on the tower. After he came down, I climbed up.

The umbrella that provided shade started rattling as the wind began to gust. I looked at the sky. The clouds were growing darker. Not good.

Just rain. Just rain. Just rain.

I heard the roll of thunder. In orientation, we were taught: "If you see it, flee it; if you hear it, clear it."

I wasn't the only one to give three short bursts on my whistle. "Out of the pool!" we all started yelling.

I could hear whistles blowing throughout the park. Water is a conduit for electricity. If lightning hits a pool, it can hurt or kill someone.

I heard a drop of water hit the umbrella. And then another.

After everyone was out of the pool and we all did a last visual scan of the water, we climbed down from our towers and headed to the pavilion. By the time we got there the rain was coming down heavily. The park had several covered pavilions and people headed to them when it rained. They weren't the safest place. But there were too many people and not enough buildings. The wise people went into the various souvenir shops, mini-restaurants, or into the locker rooms.

It was eerie once all the yelling stopped, and people weren't rushing down slides or through tubes any longer. There was a hushed silence as people waited. The scent of rain mingled with chlorine.

"So are we going to get a refund?" Michael asked from behind me.

I wondered how Michael had managed to find me in the crowd. Of course, I guess I stood out in my red swimsuit and visor. Or maybe not. There were several lifeguards around. I didn't want to be glad that he seemed to take an interest in me, but I was.

"Depends how long it rains," I told him, glancing over my shoulder. "It has to rain an hour and a half. And you don't get a refund; you get a rain check, which means you can come back another day without paying."

Someone would just stand at the gate handing out rain checks as people left.

"I know what a rain check is," Michael said.

I shrugged. "I don't know what you know."

"Doesn't seem fair. I mean, we just got here a little while ago."

"Should have gotten here sooner. It was beautiful this morning."

"I didn't see any lightning just now."

"Thunder means lightning was somewhere."

"But not close enough."

"Lightning isn't predictable. You can't take chances."

He shifted around so he was standing beside me, almost in front of me. "Want to go get a Coke?"

I almost said, "What? With you?" Instead, I very practically said, "I'm working."

"No, you're not. You're waiting for the storm to pass over."

"I have to make sure people don't go back to the pool until it's safe."

"You really take your job seriously."

I couldn't tell if he thought that was a flaw in my character.

"Sure. Don't you take your work with the lights seriously?" I asked.

"Yeah, I guess."

The rain suddenly stopped. People started moving out.

Trent blew his whistle. "Y'all have to wait thirty minutes after the last roll of thunder sounded. We've got twelve minutes to go."

People grumbled, but they also started to relax. Waiting out a storm causes a tenseness because we're crammed together, with nothing fun to do.

"He's worse than you," Michael said.

"He's doing his job."

"So what made you want to work here anyway?"

"I love the water," I confessed.

"Playing around it, I can see. But working around it?"

"I just like it. I wish I lived on the coast or on a tropical island." I nodded as I realized my preference. "A tropical island would be better."

"Have you ever been to an island?" Michael asked.

I shook my head. "Nope. This is the closest I've ever come."

"Me, too. Maybe someday . . ."

I wondered if he was hinting that maybe someday we'd go to an island together. Yeah, right. And Jasmine would spoon-feed us ice cream.

Trent blew his whistle. "Okay!"

Everyone screamed, yelled, and started running for the pool.

"I gotta get back to work," I told Michael.

"Maybe I'll see you when you take a break later."

"What about Jasmine?"

"What about her?"

"I thought you were ice-cream buddies."

"Not really."

Did I want to take a break with him? Was I treading in dangerous water?

"Morgan!"

I spun around. Trent jerked his thumb toward the pool.

"I was just on my way."

I hurried past him, feeling so stupid. Model employee had suddenly turned into Miss Get-in-trouble-whenever-she-can.

Still, I was actually thinking about taking a break with Michael. What would it hurt?

Tanner came to relieve me when it was time for my break. He gave me the smile that caused a dimple to form in his cheeks on either side of his mouth. When I'd first met him, I'd thought it was the cutest. I'd wondered if he had the dimples when he kissed. I'd been anxious to find out. But we'd never kissed. Now I couldn't have cared less about his dimples.

"So how are the plans for the Fourth coming along?" he asked as I stepped down from the platform.

"We're not allowed to talk about them. They're very hush-hush."

"Really?"

"Would I say it if it wasn't true?" I wiggled my fingers at him and walked toward the deck.

Michael met me there.

"Break?" he asked.

"Break."

He grinned. He didn't have Tanner's adorable dimples, but his smile seemed more sincere. "How about the food court? I need my afternoon smoothie energizer," he said.

While I found us a table, he got us each a tropical smoothie.

"Thanks," I said, before taking a sip on mine. "So how's the light show coming along?"

"Pretty good."

"Whitney said you were going to set some things up tomorrow night."

"No big deal. Dad just needs to get the lay of the land, so to speak. I don't really want to talk shop."

"What do you want to talk about then?"

"I don't know. Tell me about Caitlin."

I laughed. "You make it sound like she's someone who isn't sitting right here."

"You're avoiding the topic."

I shrugged, sipped some smoothie. "Not a lot to say, really."

"You have a boyfriend?"

Okay, he apparently didn't have a problem diving into deep water. "Nope."

"Someone you like?"

"I like a lot of people."

"Seriously." His voice was a little stern, but I didn't want to play seriously.

"Seriously. I like Robyn and Whitney —"

"A guy. Are you interested in a guy? Like that lifeguard that watches you all the time?"

I almost choked on my smoothie. "What lifeguard?"

"I heard someone call him Tanner."

I scoffed. "We are so over."

"So he was your boyfriend?"

I was flattered that he thought I had a boyfriend, that he thought other guys were interested.

"No. Tanner and I hung around together for a while, but it wasn't anything." I was impressed by my ability to make it sound as though it had never been anything. Maybe I was really over him. I leaned forward, tired of talking about me. "So how did your dad get into lights?"

"Okay, that wasn't a very subtle change in topics."

"I just don't want to talk about me. I'm feeling boring these days."

He grinned. "You're not boring. As a matter of fact, there's usually excitement when you're around."

"Yeah, right. So much excitement that people are calling me whistle-blower and *not* in a flattering way."

"Ouch!"

"Exactly. So your dad?"

Michael shrugged. "He used to be in a band —"

"What? You mean like a play-music-go-on-tour kind of thing?"

He grinned. "Yeah. They even cut an album, but it never amounted to much. But they'd do all this light stuff as part of the show and after a concert, people came up to the stage more interested in the light show they'd seen than in the music they'd heard. So Dad decided maybe his talent rested in lights instead of bass guitar."

"I've never known anyone in a band."

"You still don't." His grin grew.

"I almost do. Do you play music?"

"Nah, I'm kind of a computer geek, which works since the light show starts with the computer." He angled his head. "What's wrong?"

I probably appeared stunned. Hadn't I told Robyn that I wanted a geek?

"You don't look like a geek."

He laughed. "What does a geek look like?"

"Geeky." Not cute, not tan, not hot. Not like Michael Romeo.

"I'm all about designing stuff on the computer," he said.

We talked a little more. He designed the Lights Fantastic Web site, created trailers for books he enjoyed reading and posted them on YouTube. It sounded neat and interesting. I was going to have to rethink what I considered geeky.

I looked at my watch. "I need to get back to work. Thanks for the smoothie."

When I got back to my station, Tanner climbed down.

"So who was the guy?" he asked.

"Not your business."

I climbed to the platform and took my seat.

I hadn't planned to use Michael Romeo to get back at Tanner, but I had to admit that it felt pretty good that Tanner noticed.

* * *

"So what's your problem lately?" Sean asked me after we got home.

We were in the kitchen. I was looking over the pizza coupons. Mom had left us a note. She and Dad had gone to a movie. Sean and I were supposed to fend. Fend meant call out for pizza.

"What do you mean?" I asked. He liked meat on his pizza. I liked vegetables, and since it was National Catfish Day, I was thinking of ordering cinnamon sticks to celebrate the holiday. I deserved a treat after the past few days.

"Trent said you've been goofing off. That doesn't sound like you."

"What? Trent doesn't sound like me? I wouldn't think so since he has a guy's voice and I have a girl's voice." I held up a flyer. "How 'bout half pepperoni, half mushrooms?"

"Just order a large all meat and a medium all vegetable."

I knew I could distract him with food. I placed the order. And what was Trent doing telling on me anyway? I know people have the impression that girls are gossips, but I swear boys are, too. And sometimes I think they're worse because they aren't as up front about it as girls, so the general population doesn't know how much they gossip. I've listened at Sean's bedroom door enough times to know that he really does talk about other people — a *lot*.

I grabbed my latest teen mag from the stack of mail that had arrived that afternoon. I loved reading teen mags, taking the tests. I'd learned a lot of things. I knew I was outgoing, felt comfortable talking to guys, and was ready to be kissed. I plopped down on the couch in the living room.

If the pizza wasn't going to arrive in twenty minutes, I would have gone up to my room. But what was the point?

The couch groaned as Sean dropped down on it. "Come on, Caitlin. Trent said you've been talking to a bunch of guys."

"A bunch? How about two? And it's really not any of your business."

"It reflects on me if you're not doing your job."

I looked over the top of my magazine. "I'm doing my job. I wasn't even on duty yet when I was talking to Tanner yesterday."

He grimaced. "Tanner? Do you like him again?"

"No. I don't like anyone. If you're talking to a girl, does it mean you like her?"

"Forget it."

"Okay." I wasn't usually this agreeable around Sean, but since I didn't want to discuss the subject —

"There's a test in here that let's you determine how well you know your girlfriend. Want to see how you score?"

He laughed and got up. "No, thanks. I think I know Robyn well enough."

I didn't know why, but it was as though a little jolt went through me. A little reality shifting. I knew he and Robyn were hanging out together —

"Do you really think of her as your *girlfriend*?"

He furrowed his brow. "Well, yeah. You didn't know that?"

I shrugged. "I guess I thought . . . I don't know. It's just weird."

"Yeah, I know. I liked her for a long time. It's just that she was your friend."

"*Is* my friend," I emphasized.

"Are y'all hanging out tomorrow?"

"Yep."

"Doing what?"

"I have a feeling we'll end up doing whatever Whitney wants to do."

After supper, I was in my room taking a test in one of my teen mags: Does your guy friend know you like him? Not that I had a guy friend that I liked, but if I ever did, I wanted to be prepared to make the right moves.

I also thought that knowing the key to letting a guy know that I liked him might also provide the key to making sure that a guy realized that I didn't like him.

My cell phone rang. I grabbed it, glanced at the display, and grinned. "Hey, Robyn. What's up?"

"I've been thinking about tomorrow, about what we want to do."

"Yeah?"

"It sounds insane, I know it does, but —"

"You want to go to Paradise Falls."

I heard her gasp. "How did you know?"

I laughed. "Because I've been thinking the same thing. Every summer, where did we go if we wanted to have fun?"

"Paradise Falls." She groaned. "But we work there. My mother doesn't hang out in her office on the weekends."

"Her office doesn't have awesome slides."

"True. Then we have that silly committee meeting tomorrow night."

"Silly? I thought you wanted to be on this committee."

"Only because of Whitney."

"Speaking of Whitney, will she be okay with your plan?" I asked.

"Since she's moved to parties and entertainment, she hasn't really had time to work on her tan. I bet she'll go with us."

"Great." And I almost meant it sincerely instead of sarcastically.

"It'll be fun," Robyn said.

"Of course."

CHAPTER NINE

Since Robyn and I hitched a ride with Sean, we got to the water park before it opened so we were able to choose the best-placed lounge chairs. Sean was shocked that we wanted to spend the day at the water park.

"Don't you get enough of it?" he asked.

"Working here, yeah, playing here, no," I told him.

Robyn and Sean were going to meet up when he took his lunch break. Right now, Robyn and I were stretched out on the lounge chairs, soaking up the rays, waiting for the park to open so we could head for the slides.

I was wearing a red bikini that I'd bought earlier in the summer. It was actually a little embarrassing because my tummy was so pale and my tan lines didn't match on my shoulders.

"I hadn't considered I'd look like some sort of strange jigsaw puzzle," I said.

Robyn laughed. "Yeah, I know."

She was wearing a bikini, too. Hers was black and white.

"Maybe we shouldn't have waited so long to do this," I said.

"I don't think anyone will notice."

I heard the park coming to life, the water start rushing over the slides in the distance. It was even better listening to everything when I knew I wasn't going to have to be responsible for anyone today.

"I have a confession to make," Robyn said.

I slid my gaze over to her. She was watching me. She looked so serious.

"I wanted to come here today because I wanted to spend a little time with Sean. Isn't it awful? That I don't want to go hours without seeing him?"

"That's what I figured. I'm not totally clueless about relationships."

Robyn sat up. "We need to find you a boyfriend."

"When school starts."

"Isn't there anyone you like? Even just a little?"

"I like you."

Even though she was wearing sunglasses, I knew she was rolling her eyes. "You're hopeless."

Not totally hopeless. I was sorta hoping that maybe Romeo would be here today. And maybe I'd see him and maybe —

"I can't believe this is what you guys wanted to do today," Whitney said as she dropped her bag beside a lounge chair and sat on it. "I was thinking spa. Complete treatment, head to toe."

Robyn laughed. "Not on my budget."

"I would have treated. Or my dad would have anyway. But too late now. I already sent the chauffeur on his way. So we're stuck here."

"Not a problem," I said. "This is really what I wanted to do."

"And why is that?" Whitney asked.

"No reason."

"Yeah, sure."

The bells clanged signaling the park's opening. I almost jumped up to head to my station. Habits were hard to break.

"I'm going to head to Screaming Falls," Robyn said.

It was an awesome ride. The guest went up several flights of stairs, stepped into an elevator, and the floor dropped out.

Of course so did the guest. Down the slide he plummeted.

"I'm up for that," Whitney said.

"Think I'll lounge around here for a while," I said. "See if I can tan my tummy just a little."

"Just in case 'no reason' shows up?" Whitney asked.

She could be so irritating.

"I don't know what you're talking about," I said.

"Whatever." She stood up, then leaned down. "I saw him waiting in line."

I almost said "*who?*" but what was the sense in dragging this out? I grabbed her arm. "What do you know about him?"

"Him?" Robyn asked. "Who are we talking about?"

"Michael Romeo," Whitney said, grinning like the Cheshire Cat. "Right?"

"You like him?" Robyn asked me. "Why didn't you say something?"

"I don't know if I like him. I just . . . I don't know. He seems nice. But he and Jasmine were eating ice cream together so . . . I don't know." It seemed like I didn't know much.

"You're way cuter than she is," Whitney assured me.

Shock of shocks. A compliment for me from Whitney. The earth might stop spinning.

"Thanks, but other factors are in play

here. Tanner kissed her. So maybe Romeo is interested in her, too." I waved all that away. "What do you know about him?"

"Just what you know — he's helping his dad with the light shows. I also know he takes care of his younger brothers while his parents are working. That's about it."

"You're not much help."

"Excuse me, but I'm not matchmeup dot com."

"I don't want to be matched up."

"Yeah, right."

I almost protested again, but like I said, we'd studied Shakespeare in English last year so I knew that it was suspicious if someone protested too much. So I let it go.

Robyn and Whitney headed for the slides and I stayed where I was. I caught Tanner looking my way once. I took some satisfaction in that, wondered what he thought. Then I realized that my being there with two girls probably wasn't going to make him regret kissing Jasmine instead of me. Wondering why I cared what he thought,

I closed my eyes. Maybe coming here today had been a mistake.

"You took my lounge chair again."

I opened my eyes. Romeo was sitting on the chair beside mine.

He grinned and pointed. "My Birks, right there."

"I've heard that before."

"Honest. These are my Birks."

I looked down and laughed. His Birks were under my chair. His feet were still in them.

He leaned forward. "What are you doing here today? You're not in uniform."

"My day off. Where else can I get fun, sun, and lots of water? Do you come here every day?"

"Pretty much. We have season passes so we want to make the most of them. Keeps my younger brothers out of trouble."

"Do they get into trouble a lot?"

"Sometimes."

He looked around the area at the tote

bags, towels, and flip-flops scattered over the chairs. "So you're here with someone."

It was a statement that sounded a little like a question.

"Whitney and Robyn. They headed to Screaming Falls," I told him.

"Why didn't you go? Does it scare you?"

His voice held a challenge. And I wasn't going to tell him the real reason that I hadn't gone. That I'd hoped he would show up. I wasn't even sure I had realized that was the reason until he *did* show up. I was really glad to see him.

"Noooo, it doesn't scare me."

"Prove it." He stood up. "Go ride it with me."

I popped up off the lounge chair and gave him a cocky grin. "Anytime."

He slipped off his Birks and tucked them under my lounge chair.

"Let's go," he said.

Before I could say anything, he took my hand and led us toward Thrill Hill.

* * *

The line at Screaming Falls was way too long. It was at least an hour and a half wait so we headed over to Blackout. It was a twisting, turning tube, dark on the inside. The inner tubes were two-seaters so people could go down in pairs if they wanted. I'd never gone down it with a guy before. I was trying not to be nervous.

"So what do I call you?" I asked as we were standing in line.

"Cute."

I laughed. *"What?"*

"Exactly. What kind of question was that? 'What do I call you?'"

"Well, I mean, I hear people calling you Romeo and no one calling you Michael so . . . I know you said Romeo was kinda embarrassing, but did you mean it?"

"Yeah, I really like Michael better."

I was a little disappointed, because Romeo had started to grow on me.

As we stood there, not talking, I was feeling sort of out of my element. I'd gone down some of the water park slides once with a guy. With Tanner. I didn't want to keep thinking about him. I didn't want to compare Michael to him. Whitney was right. I shouldn't judge Michael based on my experience with Tanner.

"What grade will you be in?" I asked.

"Eleventh."

"So you're sixteen?"

"Yep."

"Have a car?"

He grinned. "Why do girls always ask that?"

"Do they?"

"Yeah. Like that girl I met the other morning, the one who sat on my shoulders? She asked me my name, then asked if I had a car. I think she wanted me to drive her someplace — but I couldn't leave, because of the twins. I think that's the reason she stopped hanging out with me."

"That must have hurt," I said.

"Not really. I mean, she was fun, but I don't know. We didn't connect."

The line was moving up slowly. We talked about school a little more. We went to the same high school, but with more than two thousand students, surprise, surprise, we'd never seen each other. Then we were at the front of the line.

"You go first," Michael said.

I sat on the front of the inner tube. Michael got on behind me and put his arms around my pale stomach. I looked down. He was so tanned. His arms were so warm that I thought I might actually get a tan from them. My mouth went dry, which was kind of crazy with all this water rushing down the slide. We were at the top of the tunnel, staring into the black abyss. A red light was blinking at the top of the tunnel.

I took a deep breath —

The light turned green and an attendant shoved us down.

I screamed as we hurtled down the tube. Michael laughed and his laughter tickled my ear and made me laugh, even while I was screaming. It was such a rush.

We emerged into the sunlight and skidded across the water. We toppled over. Then we got up and waded out of the pool. Michael was pulling the inner tube behind him. Then he tossed it onto the conveyor belt that carried it back up to the top of the slide.

"That was awesome," he said.

"You say that like you've never ridden it before."

"I haven't. I usually hang out at Tsunami so the twins can find me if they need me."

I was stunned. "Is this the first year you've come here?"

"Yep. First year I've had a car. My parents were never around to bring us, so you know . . ."

There was another "you know" that I really didn't know. My mom or Robyn's mom would usually bring us on the weekends. Sean was always there to make sure that we were okay. I'd never really thought about how much he actually looked after us. Then when he got his license he started to bring us. I really was going to have to stop seeing him as evil.

"Well, in that case," I said, "I may have to insist that you do Screaming Falls."

"But the wait is at least an hour."

"It's worth it. And I know all sorts of jokes."

I didn't really. As we stood in line, I tried to remember what sorts of clues the test I'd taken the night before had indicated would let a guy know I liked him. One was to smile whenever he touched me, even if it was accidental. The problem there was that we weren't touching.

We talked about movies, we talked about music, we talked about TV shows. We were almost to the top when we heard an announcement:

"Michael Romeo, please come to the Castaway Hut. Michael Romeo, please come to the Castaway Hut immediately."

That was so not good. The Castaway Hut was where lost or frightened kids — or terrified parents who couldn't find their kids — went.

"I've got to go," Michael said.

He started making his way back down the stairs. I followed him. Oddly, people weren't moving aside, not until he said, "Excuse me."

A few people said, "Hey, you're going the wrong way, dude." Some laughed.

I think they thought he'd chickened out at the top. It happened. This ride was probably the scariest in the park. But I knew he wasn't scared. He was just being a good brother.

He was moving really fast, and I could barely keep up.

Once he got to the bottom of the stairs, he finally looked back. "You don't have to come."

"Sure I do. It's probably nothing," I said. "One of them probably just got lost."

Only it wasn't one of them. It was both of them. And they hadn't gotten lost. They'd gotten hungry.

CHAPTER TEN

"You don't have to hang around while I feed the munchkins," Michael said.

We were sitting at a table in the food court while his brothers scarfed down cheese dogs — which were basically corn dogs except they had cheese instead of meat inside. Quite honestly, they were gross, almost as bad as the blue hot dogs.

"What are friends for?" I asked. According to the test I'd taken, I was supposed to say something else that hinted that I wanted to be more than friends. But I couldn't remember what it was. Maybe because being this close to Michael was distracting. He really had the most mesmerizing eyes. I always thought of blue eyes as being gorgeous. But his were so different that I couldn't stop staring at them.

He'd taken his sunglasses off before we'd hit the rides. He'd gone to his guest locker to get some money, but the sunglasses were back where I'd left my things by the lounge chair. Fortunately, the table we were sitting at had an umbrella that provided shade.

"I'm supposed to stay at Tsunami if I don't want to follow them around. So they can find me easily." He grimaced. "And it's the place Mom worries about the most so she never wants them playing there without me watching them. I guess I'm lucky it was just hunger pains and not something serious that had my name being announced across the park."

At least now I knew why he hung around Tsunami. I'd started to think that maybe I was the attraction. I really needed to stop giving myself so much credit for attracting guys. "My granddad is always telling me not to borrow trouble. You should take his advice. Nothing bad happened. So we can hang out with them —"

"You're going to hang out with us?" one of the twins asked.

"Only if we stop at the tattoo booth and get your names tattooed on your foreheads so I know who is who."

The boys giggled. I really couldn't tell them apart.

"But it's your day off. You watch kids all week," Michael said.

"I don't play with them." Then I remembered that old Shakespeare saying about protesting too much. "Unless you don't want me hanging around."

"No, that'd be great. Seriously."

"Can we go on the forbidden rides then?" one of the twins asked.

I laughed. "The forbidden rides?"

"The red rides," Michael said. "They're not allowed on the red rides."

The park had a rating system. Each slide, tube, or ride had a border around its sign to indicate the thrill level. Green was mild — slow and easy. Yellow was moderate — a little faster, some turns, a rush. Red was warning — fast, high, drops, dips, strong swimmers only, screams anticipated.

"We'll do one," Michael said. "Then we'll see how you feel after that." He looked at me. "So what would be a good starter ride for boys who want to experience an adrenaline high?"

We headed to Whirlpool — after we had the twins' names tattooed on their arms in a medieval-looking font. The temporary tattoo booth provided water-resistant tattoos, so they lasted a little longer than regular face painting.

"This is awesome," Tony said.

"I'm not going to scream," Tommy said. He looked at me. "Will you scream?"

"Definitely."

The boys were cute and having them

with us chased away any awkwardness that Michael and I might have felt while we were waiting in line. Of course, having them around also stopped him from holding my hand. Probably because he didn't want to hear them singing about us sitting in a tree, K-I-S-S . . .

But it was a little hard not to think about kissing him.

He was nice and so patient with his brothers. I think I'd taken a test once that gave boys points for being nice to kids and dogs. It reflected their true inner self or something. Maybe I was relying on tests too much. Maybe I should just go with my gut instinct.

The line didn't move too slowly since it was loading four people at a time. The slowest ones loaded only one person at a time.

"You know, if I built a water park, I think I'd make it all elevators, escalators, and moving walkways," Michael said.

"But then we'd all be out of shape and

we wouldn't have the lung capacity for a great scream when we went down the slides," I teased.

He grinned. He really had a terrific grin. "Good point. And we need those screams."

When we got to the top, all four of us hopped into the four-person inner tube — which reminded me a lot of a four-leaf clover. Michael was beside me. His arm brushed mine. I smiled at him. *Show you're interested. Smile if his hand grazes over yours.* The test had said something like that. I figured an arm brushing against mine was even better.

Then we were plummeting down the slide and I wasn't thinking about grazing hands or brushing arms. I was just thinking about holding on for dear life.

The twins loved it, loved it, loved it. They wanted to do Screaming Falls next so we got in line for that ride. The line was even longer than before.

"Don't you have a cut-to-the-front-of-the-line pass or something?" Michael asked.

I shook my head.

"There must be some benefits to working here."

I almost said, "I met you." But how corny was that? And even though I was thinking that maybe Whitney and Robyn were right and I shouldn't judge Michael based on Tanner, I also worried that maybe he was too nice. Were some guys really this nice?

"Well, hey you!" Jasmine said with a big grin when we got to the top of the slide. She pushed Michael's shoulder as though she was used to getting personal with him. "About time you came to see me."

Had he known this was the slide she worked at? Was that the reason that he'd wanted to come here? I had a strong urge to step forward and say, "He's with me."

But he wasn't really *with* me. We were just hanging out together.

"Why don't you go first?" Michael suggested to me. "Then the twins can go. That way someone they know is waiting down there for them."

"Sure." His suggestion made me feel important. Like he trusted me. I smiled at Jasmine right before I stepped into the booth. I crossed my arms over my chest, watched as Michael and Jasmine talked and laughed while she kept touching him. I wanted to scream —

And then I was screaming, for real. The floor had dropped out and I was rushing down the slide. I hit the water, bounced back to the surface. I swam to the side where a lifeguard helped me climb out.

"Hey, don't you work here?" he asked.

"Yeah. Day off."

"Man, why would you hang around here?"

The truth was that I no longer knew.

"Are you okay?" Michael asked.

We were floating in inner tubes along the Sometimes Raging Rapids. The twins needed to take it easy for a while after the exhilarating rides. They were up ahead of us in their own tubes. Michael and I were holding hands — so we stayed together. Otherwise, we had little control over where the tubes went.

"Yeah, I'm fine."

"Are you sure, because you seem —"

"Okay, did you know Jasmine was working that ride?"

"What? No."

"Are you seeing her?"

He looked surprised. Which I thought was a good thing. Unless it was fake.

"It's hard not to see her when she's standing right there."

I groaned. "You know what I mean."

"Yeah, I guess I do, and no, I'm not."

The only thing worse than multiple questions are multiple answers, because now I had to back up and attach them to the questions.

"Are you jealous?" he asked.

"No." I said that too quickly and loudly. That old protesting-too-much thing.

Grinning, he dipped my hand in the water and pulled me closer until out tubes bumped. I wasn't sure why, but he suddenly seemed very happy.

After we finished going around the park twice in the meandering river — not taking the roaring rapids detour either time — Michael and his brothers had to leave. I was disappointed, but I needed alone time to do some serious thinking.

When we got back to the lounge area, Michael slipped on his Birks.

"Thanks for hanging around with us today," he said.

"Sure. I had fun."

It looked as though he wanted to say something else, but then the twins started singing the only song it seemed like they knew, the song about Michael and me.

Michael swung around. "I'm gonna kill you guys!"

They shrieked and ran off toward the entrance.

"No running!" I yelled after them automatically.

Chuckling, Michael turned back to me. "I'd better go. See you later tonight."

"Right." The team meeting. I wasn't dreading it any longer.

I watched him walk away. Then I sat on my lounge chair and stretched out. My tummy was feeling a little tight. I looked down. Did I get sunburned?

"Where have you been all day?" Robyn asked as she and Whitney came to stand over me. They were eating ice cream, which unfortunately made me think about Jasmine.

"And whose Birks were snuggling with your flip-flops?" Whitney asked, wiggling her eyebrows.

"Wouldn't you like to know?"

"Well, yeah, that's why I asked." Whitney sat on the foot of my lounge chair so I had to pull my legs back.

Robyn sat on the lounge chair beside me. "So really, who was it?"

I glanced around. "You can't say anything."

"Geez, what is he? A spy or something? James Bond?" Whitney asked.

I scowled at her. "No, it's just that it's all new and it might not be anything and I don't want to jinx it if it is."

"Sounds serious," Whitney said.

"That's just it." I couldn't keep the frustration out of my voice. "I don't know if it's serious. But it probably isn't. He was flirting with another girl so —"

"Whoa, whoa, whoa, back up," Robyn said. "First of all, who's the guy?"

"Michael Romeo."

Her mouth dropped open. "Oh."

"Well, what do you know? I am matchmeup dot com. I get credit for this matchup," Whitney said.

"You know, Whitney, it's not always about you."

"Of course it is."

I shook my head. Why did I even like her?

"No, seriously," Whitney said. "What happened? Did you take a tube ride through the Tunnel of Love?"

"No. We watched his brothers most of the day."

"You babysat? Where's the romance in that?" She sounded appalled.

"That's just it. I don't know if there's any romance. We were just hanging out together. Quite honestly, I think our shoes got closer together than we did."

"Nothing wrong with taking it slow," Robyn said. "Especially if he's flirting with someone else. What was that about?"

I told them about Jasmine.

"I should kick her off the team," Whitney said.

"No," I said. "He either likes me or he doesn't."

"I think you just have all these doubts because of Tanner," Robyn said.

"Probably."

"Want some ice cream?" Robyn asked, holding her cup of strawberry toward me.

"Well, it is Carpenter Ant Awareness Week."

Robyn laughed while I took a bite of her ice cream. It was so good. How could I stay glum with wicked ice cream melting in my mouth? Robyn never went for the sugar-free because she didn't see the point. If she was going to be bad, she was going to be bad all the way. Of course, she wasn't a calorie magnet like I was.

"What are you talking about? Carpenter ants?" Whitney asked.

"I ration my sugar intake by only eating sweet stuff on holidays."

"You, my friend, are mental."

She moved to her own lounge chair and stretched out like a contented cat.

"Seriously," Robyn said in a low voice, "don't project Tanner onto Michael."

Part of our health class last year dealt

with mental health. Robyn had loved it, so she sometimes talked like a psychiatrist or something.

"Michael seems really nice," she added.

Yeah, he did.

Now I just had to figure out what that meant for me.

CHAPTER ELEVEN

Since we had a late meeting, we headed home to eat and change clothes. Sean was bringing us back and attending the meeting because he was "special" — or at least he was according to Robyn. And he was our ride.

I thought we probably could have gotten Whitney to give us a ride in her chauffeur-driven limo but I really didn't have a problem with Sean being there. It wasn't as if we were some secret group, doing something we weren't supposed to do. Besides, he'd already designed the advertisement that they'd put on the Paradise Falls Web site about our exciting Fourth of July Extravaganza and light show. It probably wouldn't hurt for him to see exactly what we were getting.

I was wearing a denim skirt, red top, and heeled sandals. I'd used a styling gel so my hair spiked here and there. It didn't look punk. I just didn't want it totally flat.

Sean was in black jeans and a black T-shirt, but he always wore black when he wasn't working.

During the week my curfew was eleven, but this was a business meeting. Mom made an exception. So did Robyn's mom. Sean and I picked Robyn up on our way back to the water park. She was wearing blue capris and a flowing tie-dyed T-shirt. I felt a little overdressed, but all Michael had ever seen me in was my bathing suit.

I didn't want to care about what he thought, but I did.

It was eerie when we got to Paradise Falls. Lights were on in the parking lot, but the lot was almost deserted except for a couple of cars, a truck, an SUV, and the white limo. Sean parked in the front row as close to the gate entrance as he could get. Except for the cars streaking by on the nearby expressway, everything was really quiet.

"This is creepy," Robyn whispered.

"I know," I whispered back. "I've never been here this late."

"Why are y'all whispering?" Sean asked in a voice that was almost a shout because everything else was so quiet.

"Just seems like we should," I said as we headed to the gate.

Sean swiped his card, the gate unlocked, and we all walked through.

"Evening," the guard announced.

I nearly leaped out of my skin, but at least I didn't release a little cry like Robyn did. Sean chuckled low.

If they weren't seeing each other, I think he might have given her a hard time.

The parrot brawked as we walked by. I jumped, but since only a few lights were on, I didn't think anyone noticed.

As we headed to Tsunami, it was like

strolling along a neighborhood street. A little light, a lot of shadows. I could see, though, that Sean and Robyn were holding hands. It made me wish that I had someone to hold my hand.

"There you are!" Whitney called out when we were nearer to Tsunami. "I didn't think you were ever going to get here."

I saw Jake standing near Whitney. I groaned when I saw Jasmine. She was standing at the water's edge, away from everyone else. She was wearing really short shorts and a halter top. Suddenly, I was second-guessing what I'd decided to wear. Was it obvious that I wanted to impress Michael? And would he even notice when Jasmine looked like a tropical island girl?

"So where's Lights Fantastic?" I asked.

"They're setting up some stuff. I don't think it's going to be as spectacular as I thought," Whitney said. "There's just going to be a couple of lights and his dad is going to look around, do measuring, get a feel for the place."

"I think it's good that we're here," Robyn said, obviously trying to make Whitney feel better about wasting our time. "It's important for the team to be involved."

"That's what I thought," Whitney said.

"It's really strange when there aren't a lot of people around," I said.

"I like it," Whitney said. "I wonder what would happen if we built a fire on the sand like they do on a real beach."

"The fire marshal would fine us," Sean said.

"Mr. Practicality," Whitney teased.

At least I thought she was teasing. She never seemed upset with my brother. He was never upset with her either, even when she did things she wasn't supposed to do. He made excuses for her. He never did that for me.

Green lights suddenly shot up into the sky like a spotlight.

"Oh, awesome!" Jasmine yelled out.

I wished I'd yelled a compliment. It wasn't like me to be so unsure. But between

Tanner dumping me, and Trent getting after me for the little things, I was feeling bruised.

The lights circled around, crossed each other. They went down, up. It was as though they were following actors on a stage that no one else could see. Then they went out. Show over.

"Is that it?" I asked.

"I don't know," Whitney said. "They said it wouldn't take long."

"We drove all the way back over here for this?"

"What did you want? The real light show?" Whitney asked.

"I wanted more than two towers of light."

"Oh, there's going to be more," Whitney said.

She said it as though she was holding something back — which, knowing Whitney, she probably was. She was the princess of surprises.

I heard a scraping sound. Someone was walking along the pool border where the lifeguard stations were. Even though he was only in silhouette, I recognized Michael.

The identification was confirmed when Jasmine raced over to him. "That was just really, really awesome."

"Thanks," I heard him say.

The sound of someone walking over sand caught my attention. This silhouette was tall, broad.

"I've got everything I need," he said in a really deep voice.

"Thanks, Mr. Romeo," Whitney said.

"You kids have fun." He started walking off.

"Have fun doing what?" I asked.

"Didn't I tell you?" Whitney asked. "We're going to Puttin' Around."

Puttin' Around had a miniature golf course and entertainment area. It was located near Paradise Falls. As a matter of fact, a lot of people spent the day at Paradise Falls, then just headed over to Puttin' Around for more fun and games because they stayed open later.

We all arrived in our separate vehicles and met at the front door. As we walked in, I realized that it had been a while since I'd been here. I'd forgotten how loud the noise was from the video arcade room. Another area had pool tables. On one side of the building was the pizza area. At the back of the building, a short hallway led to a door that opened out onto the miniature golf course.

As Whitney started walking toward the back, I asked, "We're really going to play golf?"

She turned to me. "Well, yeah. Don't you play?"

"Sure."

"Great. My dad's paying."

She walked up to the counter to get her club and ball.

"Do you think her dad is real?" I whispered to Robyn.

"Of course."

I wasn't so sure.

A few minutes later as I stood on the green with my club and blue ball, I realized that Whitney hadn't really considered the logistics. We were an odd number, so we couldn't really play teams.

"Romeo and I can be partners," Jasmine said, winking at him.

"I don't think we need partners," I said. "We have enough equipment to go around."

"There are two courses," Whitney said. "So Robyn, Sean, Jake, and I will take that course over there and everyone else gets the other course. Okay? Great."

She started walking away. Jake followed. Robyn looked at me with an expression that said, "What do I do?"

I waved her on. Part of me wanted to go inside and find a violent video game. But I wasn't going to leave Jasmine out here with Michael. He was mine. Kind of. But nothing was official, so I understood why he didn't shove Jasmine aside. It would have been rude. He wasn't rude.

"So who goes first?" Jasmine asked.

"My dad taught me that ladies always go first," Michael said.

"We're not ladies," Jasmine said.

"Girls. Close enough," I said. "But when my family plays miniature golf, we're all equal. So here's what we do." I took them over to the putting green. "We all hit our ball against that wall, and the one whose ball rolls back and lands closest to the tee line goes first."

"Sounds fair," Michael said, a challenge in his eyes.

I had a feeling that he played a lot — just like I did.

My theory proved correct when Jasmine's ball didn't even hit the wall, but Michael's and mine came close to being even. I was just a fraction ahead.

So I went first, and sunk a hole in one. And I was feeling pretty confident when I picked up my ball from where it rolled through a tunnel to the second hole. But when I turned back and saw Michael teaching Jasmine how to hold the club, my heart sank.

The competition here didn't involve strokes. It was all about who could keep Michael's attention. If Jasmine was really as dumb about golf as she was acting, I'd eat my miniature golf ball.

Seven strokes later, she still hadn't managed to sink the ball. But she was sure having a good time, laughing about how uncoordinated she was.

"Uh, hate to be a bad sport here," I said, "but we usually play five-stroke limit."

"What does that mean?" Jasmine asked.

"If you can't get the ball in the hole in five strokes, you move on to the next hole."

"That doesn't seem fair."

"Well, the thing is, there are usually people waiting to play so you don't want to slow down the movement over the course," I explained.

She looked behind her. "There's no one waiting for the course. If you want to go ahead, go ahead. You don't have to wait on us."

No way was I going on by myself.

"Caitlin's right, Jasmine. We don't want to slow the game down and it's always more fun if you have some competition, so five strokes." He wrote the number down on the card and handed it to her so he could putt his ball in — even though he should have gone second.

It took him two strokes.

"Not bad," I said.

"Do you play a lot?" he asked.

"Oh, yeah, my dad is really into minia-ture golf. On family vacations, we always hit at least one golf course." I lined up my shot —

"You're not aiming it at the hole," Jasmine said.

"Because I'm going to hit it off the wall first," I told her. The location of the hole, the obstacle of a short wall with two holes on either end presented a challenge. But I persevered. Two shots later, I was again standing there watching the Jasmine Show.

I turned my attention to Michael. He was so patient with her. I liked that about him. That he took care of his brothers, helped his dad, and didn't seem to mind that Jasmine had to be shown what to do at every hole. Or was he pretending, too? Liking the attention she gave him.

Maybe I should *just go ahead*, I thought, because it was painful to watch her performance.

I realized it *was* a performance when we finally got to the sixteenth hole. It was a complicated setup with a narrow bridge going over a small river of rushing water and then through a little windmill tunnel where the fan was inside the tunnel so if I didn't time it just right, it knocked the ball back out. Five strokes and I couldn't get the shot I needed to drop the ball in the hole. Same thing for Michael. We both laughed at the toughness of it. Had a bonding moment, because we both realized it was a really challenging hole.

Then Jasmine went. Two shots. Over the bridge. Through the tunnel. The ball landed in the hole.

She squealed and threw her arms around Michael, hugging him. I couldn't help but think the whole game had been an act, waiting for the one minute when she could hug him.

What made it really bad was that I wanted to hug him — and shove her into the river.

When we finished our eighteen holes, we headed for the pizza shop.

"You're really good," Michael said to me.

"Thanks."

"My brothers and I play a lot," he said.

"I could tell you were a pro."

"Not really," he said, grinning. "No one pays me to play."

When we got to the pizza shop, our other group was already there. Three chairs were at the end of the table, and Michael ended up sitting between Jasmine and me. It was awkward. I didn't want to play her game. So I just ate my pizza and talked to the others. I was glad when the pizza was gone and we decided it was time to go home.

I didn't think Michael was interested in Jasmine, but I wasn't completely sure he was interested in me either. How could a girl be sure what a guy was thinking?

CHAPTER TWELVE

On Sunday night the park closed an hour early. I know an hour doesn't seem like much, but it really is. It gave us time to catch a movie or hang out at a pizza joint before we were too wiped out to do anything. It was an hour of energy that we didn't have during the week.

Thank goodness, we'd had no more committee meetings and no more surprise meetings. I thought if Whitney said one more time "Oh, didn't I tell you?" that I was going to kick her out of our circle of friends.

As I walked into the locker room, I was thinking of catching a movie, maybe even seeing if Whitney wanted to go with me. I'd probably have to invite Sean so I'd have a ride to the movie. Or maybe I could get my mom to take me. I really hated being without wheels.

Robyn had wanted to work here this summer so she could save up to get a car when she turned sixteen. I'd wanted shoes. But I was starting to think that I wanted a car. But I hated to give up shoes.

I was debating the pros and cons of each with myself as I punched in the number for my locker.

"Surprise! Party tonight!" Whitney exclaimed.

I spun around. "What? For who?"

She laughed. "For us. Anyone and everyone."

She handed me a card. "Address is on that. Get there as soon as you can."

"No, seriously, who is it for?" I asked.

"The surprise is that I'm having a party, not that it's for anyone."

She was handing out cards to anyone

who walked by. Not exactly an exclusive guest list.

"Why didn't you say something before?" I asked.

"Because I wanted it to be a surprise," she said.

Robyn walked up and Whitney handed her a card. "Surprise! It's a party tonight."

"You're crazy," Robyn said.

"Just like to party."

I liked to party, too, but if she was just passing the invitations out now, the chances were that she wasn't going to ask —

"Who all are you inviting?" I asked.

"People I know."

She knew Michael. Would she invite him or was she inviting only Paradise Falls employees? But did she know him well enough to ask him? If she did, did I want to see him again? I hadn't seen him since we'd played miniature golf. So if he was bringing his brothers here, they weren't hanging around Tsunami. So maybe he wasn't bringing his brothers — or maybe he was hanging around Screaming Falls with Jasmine.

I'd actually taken a walk over there during my break that afternoon. I was pretty pathetic. Robyn was right. It wasn't fair not to trust Michael, just because I couldn't trust Tanner.

Still, I couldn't bring myself to trust Whitney completely either. So I didn't ask her if she'd invited Michael.

Lights Fantastic had a Web site. A Web site with a phone number. Maybe it was for an office. On a Sunday night, no one would be there. On the other hand, maybe it went directly to Michael's dad and I could give him the information about the party and tell him to tell Michael.

On the other *other* hand, it wasn't my party so it would be rude to invite someone.

I was in my bedroom, staring at the Web site, wondering if my friendship with

Whitney had gotten to the point where she wouldn't be upset if I invited someone who I wanted to be there. If it was Robyn's party, no problem. I could ask anyone I wanted. But Whitney's? I just wasn't as solid with our friendship.

Plus, I had no idea what Whitney had in mind for her party. It might be boring. Maybe I wouldn't want Michael to be there.

Maybe I wouldn't go.

I had gotten dressed as though I was going to go. I was wearing a short blue skirt and a red spaghetti-strap top. Little gemstones ran along the straps and the scooped neck. I'd sprayed some glitter in my hair. I loved the sparkles, especially during party time. I was actually excited about a party.

So why was I thinking about not going?

Because I was pretty sure that Whitney invited Jake and she'd probably hang out with him. Even if she didn't, I figured he'd be giving her some attention. So Whitney would either be flirting with or avoiding Jake. Robyn would be hanging out with Sean.

And that would leave me alone. Which would be okay if I didn't have an interest in Michael.

A knock sounded on my door. "You ready?" Sean asked.

I opened the door. "I don't know if I'm going."

"Why not?"

I shrugged.

"Come on. Whitney's excited about the party. She has a surprise planned."

"What surprise?"

"Something she's been working on."

"Why do you care if she's happy?"

"Why don't you care if she is?"

"That doesn't even make sense."

"Let's go, Caitlin."

"I don't —"

"Michael's going to be there."

"How do you know that?"

"I just know. So come on."

"It's Whitney, right? You have some sort of secret friendship with her —"

"Sometimes I can't believe you're my sister. I'm going to the party."

As though he thought he'd told me all I needed to know to want to go, he spun on his heel and headed for the stairs. Or maybe he'd given up on me and figured if I was going to go that I'd follow.

He was right. I followed.

"So there's really nothing out here," I said. "Are you sure you know where you're going?"

We were driving along what horror stories referred to as a lonely country road. It was almost dark —

"According to MapQuest," Sean said.

"Oh, there!" Robyn said from the front seat. "There are some houses."

"No," I muttered. "I don't think those are houses. They're palaces."

They were huge and set back off the

main road with long winding driveways. Wrought-iron fences surrounded most of them, although some had brick walls so I couldn't see inside.

"Did you even know we had places like this around here?" I asked.

"Maybe we *are* in the wrong place," Robyn said.

"Street name is right," Sean said. "And there's the matching house number."

The wrought-iron gates were open. Brick posts were on either side of them and the house number was carved in black marble on one of them. A winding, circular driveway led to the house. Dozens of cars were already parked along the driveway and near the five-car — *five-car*! — garage. A basketball court was beside that.

"Okay," I said as Sean shifted the car into park. "It's official. She's rich. More than rich."

"This is amazing," Robyn said as we got out of the car.

"*Who* is she?" I looked at Sean. "Did you know about all this? Is that the reason you always try to make sure she's happy?"

"I know some things, but not this."

"Why don't you tell us some of those things?"

"Can't." He reached out and took Robyn's hand. "Come on. I can't wait to see the inside."

We walked up the grand, sweeping steps. It reminded me of a movie star's house or something. Sean rang the doorbell. I told myself it was just a house. No reason to be nervous.

The door opened. Whitney, smiling brightly, ushered us in.

"Where's the butler?" I asked.

She laughed. "No butler. That's so old school." She gestured to the woman beside her. "This is Aunt Sophie. She looks after things when Dad is out of town. He's in Europe right now."

Like Whitney, her aunt just looked rich. She was wearing silk lounging pants and lots of diamonds. Her hair was a blond color that was almost white. Not like my grandmother's. Not gray. Not silver, but a really white blond.

"We're starting out in the media room," Whitney said. "You guys are the last to arrive. What took you so long?"

"Caitlin," Sean said, and I wanted to hit him. Whitney didn't need to know that I hadn't wanted to come. "She couldn't decide what to wear," he finished, then winked at me.

That was a much better excuse. My brother was turning out to be better than I'd ever thought he'd be.

As we walked through the foyer, I was amazed by what I could see of the house. It was all marble and gold, and it was so big. Whitney was leading us to some wide, curving stairs. Yapping echoed in the hallway and a little white ball of fur bounded into the foyer. Whitney reached down and picked him up.

"This is Westie," she said.

"What's his name?" I asked, reaching out to pet him. He licked my hand.

"Westie."

"I thought that was his breed."

"It is, but it's his name, too."

Not very imaginative, but then I guess it worked.

Holding him close, she led us up the stairs and then down a short hallway into the media room. There were three rows of recliners, stairs leading to a balcony, stars twinkling on the ceiling, and a huge, huge screen on the front wall.

"Get comfortable. Pillows are on the floor. Mr. Romeo is going to give us a preview of the show he's working up for us."

So this was a team meeting with guests? Was Jasmine around?

Whitney headed for the stairs. I guess Mr. Romeo was operating things from the balcony. At the back of where we were standing was a waist-high wall and behind that a beverage and food bar. Little tubs of popcorn were lined up. I grabbed a couple and handed them to Robyn and Sean. They moved down to the front of the room. It was dark in here, like a movie theater. I didn't think they'd do any kissing, but I didn't want to take a chance of being close to them if they did.

The room was suddenly plunged into complete darkness. Someone shrieked. Others laughed.

Then images began appearing on the big screen. It was a video of a light show. Music blasted from speakers. It looked as though it was at a fair or something, like it was outside. I grabbed a tub of popcorn for myself and eased behind the short wall and rested my arms on it, still managing to eat some popcorn. If we had a room like this in our house, I didn't think I'd ever go to a movie theater. I loved this room.

"Pretty boring, right?" a voice whispered near my ear.

Michael. I peered over at him. "What? Oh, no. Really."

I could see his grin, even in the semi-darkness. He took my hand and led me out of the room, into the hallway.

He still spoke low. "You know, I like my dad but if you ask him to make you a sandwich, he's going to tell you how they planted the seeds to grow the wheat to make the bread."

"Is that what he's doing in there?"

"Yeah, he's trying to explain everything that goes into creating a show. But who cares? It's like a magician's trick. Just show the audience the magic. Don't show them how it's done."

"Do you know how it's done?" I asked.

"Yeah, I know how it's done. I mix the music."

I looked back toward the room we'd just come out of. "Is he going to show us what y'all have planned for the Fourth?"

"Only a little bit. Why ruin the surprise? Want to see something neat?"

Okay, we really seemed to be jumping around here. Part of me wanted to see the preview of the light show, part of me agreed with Michael and wanted to wait for the real deal. Most of me wanted to hang out with him.

"I can't imagine anything neater than what I've already seen of this house," I told him.

"Did you see her dad's vintage Mustang?"

I shook my head.

Grinning, he took my hand again and led me down a hallway.

"Is it okay for us to go this way?" I asked.

"No wonder you're a lifeguard. You worry about the rules too much."

"I do not."

He looked over at me. Well, okay, I guess I did. Some of the other lifeguards were still calling me the whistle-blower. I blew my whistle more than anyone else. Maybe the bad kids just hung out in my section of the pool.

"That was fun the other night, playing miniature golf," he said.

"You didn't really get to play much. You were an instructor."

"Jasmine took it all so seriously."

Did he really think she was trying to learn the game? I thought she just wanted to be near him.

Michael turned down another hallway. One side of it was all glass. And on a platform, like the kind in auto shops, was a car. Below it was another garage.

"Wow! That is out of control. Who displays their car like a trophy?" I asked.

"It is a trophy." Michael moved closer to the glass. "It's awesome."

Had to be a guy thing, because I was standing there thinking that a two-story shoe closet would be the way to go. Why waste all that space on a car?

"What do you know about Whitney?" I asked.

"Nothing really. She's nice."

He took my hand again. "Stairs leading outside are over here."

"Should we go outside?"

"Sure, that's where the party is going to be. According to Whitney."

We went down the back stairs. Michael opened a door and walked out onto a patio. The pool was huge, with a waterfall and a fire pit in the center of it. It was almost too much.

"I didn't bring a bathing suit," I muttered.

"I'd think you'd get enough water at the park."

"Is that what happened to you?" I asked. "You had enough with the water? I haven't seen you there lately."

"The twins came down with strep so I've had to play doctor. Boring. Try keeping those two occupied."

I was sorry to hear about his brothers, but also glad to know that I hadn't done anything to keep him away. I was such a mess. I liked him a lot more than I wanted to — and I was afraid to let him know how much.

I wanted him to make all the first moves. I wanted him to say he liked me. I wanted him to leave me with no doubts.

I knew it was unfair. I knew in relationships there had to be give and take. I saw that with my parents. And okay. Even with Robyn and Sean.

"Is your house anything like this?" I asked.

"Yeah, I live next door."

My mouth dropped open. "Really?"

He laughed. "No. No way. This is . . . well, it's almost too much, you know?"

Yeah, I did. And it made me see Whitney in a different light. I wondered if she was working at the water park because she wanted to be normal, like everyone else, because living like this wasn't the way that most of us lived.

Suddenly I heard voices and laughter. People were coming out onto the patio.

"Guess Dad's finished with show-and-tell," Michael said.

He sounded relieved. I didn't get it. It

was as though he didn't want us to have a preview of the upcoming light show. I wondered if he'd done more than the music, if maybe he'd created the show and was self-conscious about it.

I recognized a lot of the people here. Music began to play. Some people started to dance. Robyn and Sean came over.

"What did you think of the light show?" Robyn asked.

"I thought it was absolutely awesome," I said even though I hadn't seen it. I didn't want them knowing that I'd left the room early.

"I liked it," Sean said, "but there's something about fireworks on the Fourth."

"No chance of fires with the light show," Michael said. "And since we've had so little rain this summer, fire marshals are cracking down on fireworks."

"But then water isn't a problem where we are," Sean said.

"Why the hard time, man?" Michael asked.

"Yeah, Sean, what's your problem? You voted for the light show," I reminded him.

"And I still like it. I just think that I'm going to miss fireworks."

"Guess we can always come out here and shoot fireworks," I said.

"Isn't this place amazing?" Robyn asked.

"Oh, yeah." Funny that I could tell Michael what I really thought but I was afraid Robyn wouldn't understand. How had that happened? That I could tell a guy I knew only a little something that I couldn't confess to my best friend?

"I need to tell my dad something," Michael said. "I'll be back."

I watched him walk over to a tall man with curling black hair. I could see him more clearly now than I had the other night. He looked a lot like Michael — or Michael looked like him.

"Okay, you have no idea that the light show was awesome," Robyn said, "because you didn't stay. We saw you sneaking out."

Busted!

"Michael wanted to show me the vintage car. Did you see it?"

Sean narrowed his eyes. Robyn punched his arm. "Lighten up." Then she turned her attention to me. "Soooo, I'd say that Jasmine is not a problem."

"Why would you say that?"

"Because she's here and he sneaked out of the room with *you*."

My stomach knotted up. "She's here?"

"Yeah."

"Where?"

"I don't know."

We both looked around. And then I saw her. On the far side of the pool, in the shadows.

Déjà vu.

She was kissing Michael.

CHAPTER THIRTEEN

"Do you want me to go beat him up?" Sean asked.

I'd clearly underestimated my brother. The worst part of all? His offering to beat up a guy for me made me cry. I never cry and here I was all blubbery.

"I just want to go home," I said.

Robyn went to tell Whitney that we were leaving. Sean directed me through the house. I needed someone telling me where to go. Number one, because I didn't have a map of the place, and number two, because everything was blurry because of the tears.

I got into the backseat. When Sean got in the front, I said, "Why can't guys like me?"

"They like you. You just pick the wrong guys."

"So it's my fault."

"I don't know, Caitie. Guys are idiots. You know that."

The front passenger door opened and Robyn hopped in. "Let's go."

She said it the way someone would during a bank heist, trying to get away. But it worked, because Sean started the car and we headed home.

"I don't know if this will make you feel any better, but Jasmine is officially off the light-show committee," Robyn said.

She sounded so mad. Robyn didn't usually do mad. It took a whole lot to upset her. So, of course, my eyes started watering again.

"Maybe it wasn't her fault," I said.

"Does it matter?" she asked.

"I don't know. I was finally starting to trust him." I groaned. "I should have stuck to my plans. No guys until school starts. And only geeks."

No one had anything to say after that. And what could they say? I was an awful judge of guys. Absolutely awful.

Sean dropped me at home first. Guess he figured out that I just wanted to be alone. When I walked in, I could smell brownies. I went to the kitchen. Mom was sitting at the counter, reading a magazine. A pan of brownies was in the middle of the counter.

"You made brownies?"

Mom looked up and smiled. "I'm sure there is some obscure holiday that we need to celebrate."

"Meteor day," I said as I walked farther into the kitchen and sat at the counter.

Mom cut me a brownie and set it on a plate.

"How did you know I needed this?" I asked.

"Sean called, told me what happened, said you were leaving the party."

I guessed that he'd done it after I'd

gotten in the car, before he got in. Or maybe he'd done it as we were leaving and I'd been too devastated to notice.

"Want to talk about it?" Mom asked.

I shook my head. Nodded. Shook my head again.

My mom is really pretty. I didn't think she'd understand. Guys were probably always kissing her — or wanting to anyway. She and Dad started dating in high school.

"Sean isn't the jerk I thought he was." I almost choked on the words.

"I know. It's difficult being younger."

"I guess." I sighed. "Michael's a jerk and I didn't think he was." I lifted my shoulders, let them drop in defeat. "I don't know how to judge guys. I always get it wrong."

"One day you won't. One day you'll get it right."

"But when?"

"Not much longer," she said. "After all, you finally figured out the truth about Sean."

That wasn't much consolation. Because I hadn't figured out the truth about Michael.

So now I was hurting again. And it hurt worse, so much worse, than it had when Tanner had betrayed me.

On the Fourth of July, the water park was crammed with people. Every age, shape, and size. Various pavilions were reserved for family reunions. Kids were running around like crazy. It was louder than it had been all summer. The sun was out. It was hot. As long as it didn't rain, we were good.

I was sitting in my lifeguard station, watching everyone playing in the pool. I hadn't seen Michael since the fateful kiss. Whitney kept in touch with him. She usually had something to say about him when we had our committee meetings. He was busy helping his dad get all the lights set up and in sync. What we'd seen at her house was just the computer rendition. Now they had to make it work and time was short so they were working really hard.

The night before, she'd had dinner with the Romeo family. She'd invited me to go with her, but I'd forgotten to make my bed that morning so I'd needed to get home to do that.

I didn't understand why *she* didn't understand that I didn't want to have anything to do with Michael. As a matter of fact, I'd almost resigned from the committee, but in an odd way, I felt as though that would have meant that Jasmine had won. As though her kissing Michael was a sign of absolute victory.

So I stayed on the committee, went to the meetings every day, and tried to look like my heart wasn't hurting.

When I was on the lifeguard platform, I tried really, really hard not to think about Michael, not to wonder what he was doing, not to wonder what I'd done wrong. It seemed as though we were liking each other — so why had he kissed Jasmine?

Late last night, the committee had hung red, white, and blue streamers all over the pavilions. Robyn and I had wrapped ribbons around the palm trees. Today's guests received little flags to wave around. Everyone was having fun: screaming, laughing, being so loud. The noise was almost deafening.

The alarm sounded, people shrieked, the waves started up. I stood up. I felt more alert when I was standing. Trent had come by a couple of times and told us to stay on our toes. When so many people are in the pool, it's easy to miss something.

I glanced toward the shallow end. I saw a boy about seven or eight walking into the pool. He was holding one of those awful blue hot dogs. He wasn't in my zone, but I knew you weren't supposed to come into the pool eating.

"Tanner!" I yelled. He was sitting in the next lifeguard platform. But there was so much noise that he didn't hear me.

I blew my whistle. Some people in the pool looked up at me. They had guilty expressions. I wondered what they'd been doing that they weren't supposed to do. But Tanner didn't look at me. Lifeguards didn't expect to have the whistle blown at them.

The waves were getting higher and stronger. The kid was still eating his hot dog. A wave plowed into him. He went down, came back up out of the water. It looked as though he was coughing or trying to cough. He wasn't holding his hot dog anymore.

I took a quick look around my area, then looked back at the kid. Something was wrong. He was staggering, holding his throat. Why didn't Tanner see him? Where was Trent?

I knew I'd get chewed out for leaving my station, but I didn't see that I had a choice. No one else seemed to be noticing what was going on. I knew there was a chance that the kid was just goofing around — and I'd get teased about panicking again. But better me getting teased than a kid choking.

I climbed down from my station and started running toward the shallow end of the pool.

"Watch my zone!" I yelled at Tanner as I passed by his station.

"What are you doing?" he called down, but I ignored him.

When I got even with the kid, I leaped into the pool and waded to him. People were playing around him. No one seemed aware that he was choking. And he *was* choking. I could see him clearly now. People don't realize that hot dogs — if they're not properly chewed — can get stuck.

"It's okay," I yelled at the kid. "Can you talk?"

His eyes were wide. He shook his head. Not good.

I put my arms around him. I'd learned the Heimlich maneuver in first-aid class, when I was being certified to be a lifeguard. I put my fist beneath his breastbone. With my other hand, I thrust it into his abdomen. The disgusting blue hot dog went flying into the water. Someone screamed. The kid gasped, choked, started to cry. I led him out of the water, sat him down on the sand.

"You okay now?" I asked.

He nodded.

"I need you to say something."

"I'm okay."

"Never eat in a pool," I said. I knew it was probably the wrong time to get after him, but what he'd done had been really dangerous.

He nodded again.

"Where are your parents or the adult you're with?"

He pointed behind him.

"Come on. Let's get you to them."

I helped him to his feet, took a step, and nearly knocked into Trent, who was probably there to chew me out. I wasn't in the mood. "He was choking," I said.

"I saw."

"I was going to take him to his parents."

"I'll do it. You should get back to your station. No one's watching your zone."

"Oh, okay."

I turned to go.

"Morgan?"

I looked back.

Trent gave me a thumbs-up. "Great job."

I smiled broadly. "Thanks."

"You're a hero!" Robyn said.

It was later in the afternoon. Robyn and Whitney had joined me for my break. We didn't usually take our breaks together because they were so short, but they were worried about me. I hadn't seen Michael since the kiss. We all knew that any time now he'd be showing up with his dad and their crew to start setting up for the light show.

Word had spread about my rescue. I felt myself blush. "It wasn't really a big deal. I don't think I'll get news coverage."

"Do you want news coverage?" Whitney asked.

I had a feeling if I said yes that she'd make it happen. She had power. I just hadn't figured out where it was coming from. "No, I really don't."

"It's not so bad," Robyn said. "News reporters are nice."

"Not always," Whitney mumbled.

"Have you been on the news?" I asked.

"Let's just say I know some reporters who aren't nice."

"Are you nervous about tonight?" Robyn asked me.

"What's there to be nervous about?"

She made an impatient face. "Michael will be here."

"So? Jasmine can have him. I knew all along he was a Romeo, so I didn't invest my heart." I couldn't say the same thing about my pride. And okay, maybe it had hurt my heart a little — a lot. How could I start to like a guy so much in such a little bit of time?

"Well, if it isn't my hero sister!" Sean announced. He took off my visor and ruffled my hair like I was a kid.

"Hey!" I snatched my visor back from him and settled it into place.

"We brought you something special."

My heart did a little crazy thudding. First of all who was "we"? Could it be Sean and Romeo? And the something special? That could be Romeo, too.

I looked around Sean. Jake was holding a tray with ice-cream cups on it.

"It's a holiday, right?" Sean asked. "And even if it wasn't, we have a 'Celebrate Caitlin' moment."

Jake set the tray down and began handing everyone a cup of ice cream. I figured Sean had helped him because he got mine right: pistachio. And Robyn's strawberry. Sean's chocolate. But how had Jake known Whitney's? I assumed he'd chosen right for her because she gave him a bright smile. Who would have thought designer Whitney was a plain vanilla?

"My break's almost over," I said.

Sean sat between Robyn and me. "I'll tell Trent to chill."

"Can you do that?" I asked.

"Hey, I'm front office. I can do anything."

Jake sat beside Whitney.

"No ice cream for you?" I asked.

He shook his head. "I'm not sure I'll ever eat ice cream again."

Whitney laughed and extended her spoon toward him. "Come on. One little bite. You have to celebrate Caitlin's breaking the Tsunami curse."

Shrugging, he took the ice cream from her spoon.

"What's this about a curse?" I asked.

"Nothing was working for you there. You meet a guy, you lose a guy. You were doing things that seemed right, only they turned out to be wrong. Blowing your whistle, clearing the pool. Now you did the right thing. The curse is broken."

"So now she'll get a guy?" Robyn asked.

It was really embarrassing to have her ask that when my brother was around.

"I don't want a guy," I said.

"Maybe another position in the park?" Whitney asked.

"No, thanks. I like Tsunami. Yes, it has its challenges, but I think Trent will get off my case now."

"Well, if he doesn't, we'll sue him for harassment," Whitney said.

"You can't sue a supervisor for doing his job," Sean said.

"Honestly, y'all, thanks, but I really think everything is going to be okay now." Or at least it would be after tonight. But maybe with it being dark, Michael would never see me. That would be great, because I didn't want to see him.

After we finished our ice cream, we all headed back to our separate jobs. I was almost to Tsunami when Tanner moved away from a palm tree. Maybe he was taking his break, too, but it seemed as though he'd been waiting for me.

"Hey," he said. "You did great rescuing that kid. That was my zone and I didn't realize he was in trouble."

I didn't want him feeling badly about what happened with the little boy. What happened with Jasmine, sure, but he didn't need to feel guilty about the kid. "I probably wouldn't have either if I hadn't seen him carrying the hot dog. Sometimes it's hard to tell if the kids are goofing off or in trouble."

"It would have been on me if things . . . well, if it hadn't had a happy ending."

"But it did have a happy ending so no point in borrowing trouble. See ya."

I started to move past him and he stepped in front of me. "Some of us are going to go out for pizza after the park closes. Someplace that has no red, white, and blue theme. I was, well, I was wondering if you wanted to go. With us. With me."

"Why now? Because I'm a hero?"

"No. Because I heard . . ." His voice trailed off.

"Heard what?" I demanded to know.

"That guy . . . Romeo. He's with Jasmine now. I really like you. I thought maybe now that he's with her, you'd give me another chance."

Before this summer, I wanted to go out with a guy more than anything. I wanted a date. More than that, I wanted a kiss. My first kiss. I never thought that if a guy asked me out, I'd say no.

But the truth was, Tanner was nice, but he wasn't Michael Romeo. And even though Michael was with Jasmine now, and he'd never be with me, I wanted to go out with a guy who made my heart do cartwheels the way that Michael did. I wanted my first kiss to be with a guy who made my toes tingle and curl when I thought about him.

I didn't really know how to tell Tanner no. I didn't want to hurt his feelings, but I didn't want to go eat pizza with him. And I *really* didn't want him to kiss me. "Thanks, Tanner, but I have plans already."

He nodded. I think he knew it was a lie.

"Well, have fun," he said.

"I will."

He walked away toward the food court, so I figured he was still on break. It was the Fourth of July. Independence Day. I'd saved someone's life, turned down a date, said no to a guy. What else could possibly happen?

I didn't see Michael until later that afternoon. I would have been happy to never see him again, but he'd come with his dad and a crew to start setting up for the light show. And since he'd decided to display it at Tsunami, they were setting up around me.

He was wearing jeans, the Lights Fantastic T-shirt, sneakers, and the baseball cap. He came up to me while I was sitting at my station. "Hey, Caitlin. You left in a hurry the other night."

It sorta sounded as though he was asking a question. I pointed behind me at the large sign with all the rules.

"Aren't we past that?" he asked.

The alarm sounded, signaling the waves so I stood up.

"Hey, Romeo!" someone shouted. "Where do you want this to go?"

Romeo. That was a much better name for him than Michael.

"Maybe I'll see you later . . . when the show starts," he said. "Whitney said her team members didn't have to work tonight. They could enjoy the show."

So Whitney was talking to him about me? Traitor. I really needed to have a talk with her.

Out of the corner of my eye, I watched him walk away. I focused my attention on the pool. I counted heads, memorized all the different faces — anything, anything to keep me distracted, from turning to see what Michael was doing. Hammering, clanking, and banging were going on behind me.

I should have called in sick. My stomach was roiling. Maybe I was going to be sick. Then I would have to go home.

At eight o'clock a girl came to relieve me. The park had extra lifeguards who rotated around and replaced us when we went to break and lunch and now one was going to work so I could enjoy the light display.

I went to the locker room and started changing into the shorts and tank top that I'd brought. No one else was here, because no one else was getting off work. The door opened. Well, almost no one else.

"This is it! The big night," Whitney said as she practically skipped into the room. "Are we excited or what?"

I swung around, she staggered back.

"Chill!" she exclaimed.

"I don't want to chill," I told her. "I thought you were my friend."

"I am."

"You told Michael that I wasn't working tonight."

"Well, yeah. He asked —"

"You talked to him — even after what he did at your party. Even after he hurt me like he did."

She looked down at her perfectly pedicured toes nestled in her expensive leather sandals. She took a deep breath and met my gaze. "I can't *not* talk to him. I have to tell him what we want for the light show."

"Do you know what a real friend is?"

"Yeah, I think so."

"Real friends don't keep secrets from each other. You're like a surface friend, like you're pretending. You're as bad as Romeo. I don't even know your last name."

She crossed her arms over her chest, her face set in a mulish expression. "St. Clair. Go Google me if knowing my secrets is so important to you." She took a step toward me. "A true friend wouldn't need to know them. A true friend would let secrets stay secrets." She turned on her heel, started to walk out, then spun back around and pointed her finger at me as though she was Hermione and wanted to change me into something else. "Just for the record, I'm a better friend than you think."

She pushed open the door, going out as Robyn was coming inside.

"Hey, what's wrong?" Robyn asked.

"Ask your friend," Whitney said as she brushed by her.

Robyn stared after her, then she looked over at me. Cautiously she made her way toward me. "What was all that about?"

I waved my hand in frustration. "She's talking to Michael, telling him things about me like everything is all right." I shook my head. "I don't even know if I want to stay for the light show."

"But it's going to be awesome."

"But we didn't really do anything, Robyn. Lights Fantastic did all the work. This was like a faux committee or something. We weren't really needed."

Robyn sat down, straddling the bench. "We were needed. Whitney needed us. Her dad travels the world, her mom is dead. She looks for things to do, like committees, so we have a reason to hang around her because she's afraid we won't if we don't have to."

"She told you that?"

Robyn shook her head. "You know me. I'm the quiet one, the one who tries to figure things out. I figured all that out."

I sat on the bench. "She said she was a better friend than I realize. I really wouldn't like it if that was true. It would make me feel so stupid." I peered over at her. "I've finally figured out that Sean really is a better brother than I thought he was."

She smiled. "I knew you would eventually. You can come watch the light show with us." She leaned forward. "I promise no kissing if you're in the area. It really is going to be awesome."

"Okay." I closed my locker, reset the lock.

We walked outside and headed for Tsunami. Sean was standing at the edge of the pool. I recognized his silhouette. It had grown dark. The park lights were on, but they wouldn't be for long.

The announcement came on that the slides, rides, and pools were closing. People began heading for Tsunami to see the light show. Excitement was buzzing in the air.

It was obvious by the energy people were generating that they were anticipating this. I felt proud to have been part of it, even if my part was really small. I wondered where Whitney was. This was really her big moment.

It was several long minutes before her voice came over the announcement system. "Ladies and gentlemen, boys and girls, on behalf of Paradise Falls we thank you for joining us as we celebrate the Fourth of July."

The lights went out and "The Star Spangled Banner" suddenly echoed through the park while a flag of lights wavered over Tsunami. It was spectacular as we all sang the national anthem.

When the song ended, people applauded. Then the next song began. I think it was something from *Titanic*. It sounded familiar but I couldn't place it. The light show, though, was amazing. The lights were flashing in rhythm to the music. Every now and then people would *ooh* and *aah*.

It was wonderful.

I felt a tug on my hand, glanced over my shoulder. It was Michael. I could barely see him in the shadows. He put a finger to his mouth and pulled on my hand. I thought about jerking my hand free. I didn't want to miss the show. I didn't want to be with him at all. And shouldn't he be with Jasmine?

I should have refused to follow him, but I had some things I wanted to say to him. I was mad at him and my telling Whitney what I thought about true friends had put me on a roll. I wanted to tell Michael what I thought about guys who kissed other girls.

I followed him as he led me away from the pool to a place beside the pavilion. A little more light was here and I could see him more clearly.

"What do you think?" he asked.

I knew he was asking about the light show. But I wasn't thinking about it anymore. I was thinking about him. "That you are a Romeo."

"Well, yeah, duh, that's my last name."

"No. That's not what I mean. I saw you. I saw you with Jasmine."

"Yeah, I thought maybe you did. I thought maybe that was why you left."

"I thought you liked me."

"I do like you. I think you're amazing."

"Oh, please," I said, my voice low but harsh. "You kissed her."

"No, I didn't. She kissed me. Took me totally by surprise —"

"You go off to the corner of the deck, away from everyone else —"

"She said she lost her cell phone and needed help finding it."

"And you believed her?"

He sighed. "Stupid, I know. Or maybe not. Why would I think she'd lie?"

"People lie —"

"I don't," he said. "I told her I was with you."

"When did you tell her that?"

"After she kissed me. I would have told her before if I'd known that's what she was going to do."

"Yeah, right. I know you're with her now."

He shook his head as though a fly was buzzing around it. "No, I'm not. How could I be? I'm standing here with you."

"No, I mean I know you're together, as in a couple, seeing each other."

"No, we're not. I can barely stand her. Why would I want to be with her? Maybe she's telling people that we're together. But trust me, we're not."

I thought I should have felt better, but what I felt was confused. He hadn't kissed her, she'd kissed him. They weren't together.

"Look, Whitney told me about you and Tanner —" Michael began.

"What?"

I was going to kill her. Without question. Without remorse. Without mercy.

"She told me that you liked Tanner and he kissed Jasmine, so I know how things looked the other night but I promise you, I don't like her. I've never liked her. I like you.

I have ever since you first blew your whistle at me. I can even prove it. Listen."

"What?"

"Just listen." He put his hands on my shoulders and turned me around so I could see the light show.

But it wasn't the lights that caught my attention. It was the song, my favorite song: "Our Song" by Taylor Swift.

I remembered Michael asking what my favorite song was after that first team meeting.

Michael leaned close and whispered, "That was part of the show before Jasmine ever kissed me."

I turned around and faced him, doubts flourishing, even as my heart was pounding. "You're just saying that."

"Why do you think I took you out of the media room at Whitney's? I didn't want you to know, not until tonight. When it was live, when it was the real thing. I didn't want you to see it when it was just something Dad and I had put together on a computer."

"You really did this for me?" I asked.

"I really did."

"You really like me?"

He grinned. "Yeah. I'm not Tanner. I'm not going to kiss another girl. You're the only girl I want to kiss. And I really want to kiss you."

"What's stopping you?"

Apparently nothing. He leaned in and kissed me.

I was seeing lights, bright lights, an awesome light show — even though my eyes were closed. His lips were softer than I thought they'd be, and warm.

My first kiss. My favorite song was playing in the background. I felt so happy. Ecstatic.

Michael drew back.

Thunderous applause echoed around us.

I looked over my shoulder. The lights were gone. I'd missed most of the show. But I didn't care. I had Michael. And he had me.

People began heading for the exit.

"I've got to help take everything down," Michael said, squeezing my hand. "When we're finished, I don't know, maybe you and I could go grab a burger or something."

"Yeah. I need to let my brother know."

Holding my hand, he began working his way through the crowd, pulling me along after him until we got back to where Robyn and Sean were waiting. Whitney was there, too.

"It was awesome, Michael!" She wrapped her arms around him and hugged him. "Thank you, thank you, thank you."

"Not a problem. It's what we do," Michael said as soon as she let go of him. "And unfortunately, we're not finished, so I'll catch up with you later."

He squeezed my hand and went to help his dad.

"So why are you smiling?" Whitney asked.

"Because I just realized you are a true friend. Thanks for everything you did so he'd know what to say to me so I'd listen."

"That's what friends are for, right?"

"Yeah," I said. "And friends don't Google friends."

"Thanks," she said. Then she waved her hands to include everyone. "I've got things to take care of. See you tomorrow."

She walked away.

"What was that all about?" Sean asked.

"Girl stuff."

"So you and Michael —"

"We're going to go get something to eat. Y'all want to come? Because Mom probably won't let me go out with him alone until she's met him —"

"Sure," Sean said. "I'm starving. But we'll sit at different tables. Think I'll see if I can do something to help, so they can finish and we can get going."

He headed toward Tsunami.

"Okay, Sean might not need the whole story, but I do," Robyn said. "Spill it."

I told her everything that Michael had told me.

"What is Jasmine's problem?" she asked when I was finished.

"I don't know. But it doesn't matter. I've got a terrific brother, a new best friend, a best friend forever, and I've got a guy who likes me."

It didn't take them long to finish. Then Sean and Robyn and Michael and I were heading toward the entrance.

"Hey, where are you guys going?" Whitney called out.

I looked over my shoulder. Jake was with her. I had a feeling there was a story there.

"To get something to eat. Want to come?" I asked.

"Yeah, sure. Great!"

I figured with her and Jake joining us that Michael and I wouldn't end up with a table to ourselves. But that was okay.

There was still a lot of summer left, and as Michael smiled at me, I knew a lot more kisses were coming, too.

I could hardly wait.

I thought about what Robyn said about Sean being there whenever she needed him. I needed someone. And Jake was there. How could I figure it out without actually asking him?

I needed some way to test his interest in me, something that would tell me what his feelings were.

"Some of us are going out for pizza after work. Did you want to go with us?" I heard myself asking, without thinking it through.

"That's the reason you're acting funny

and thinking of working someplace else? Because you're going out for pizza?"

"I've got a lot on my mind. So do you want to go out for pizza or not?" I knew I sounded put out. Why would he be interested in me when I was so difficult? I had a feeling that he was going to fail this test. And it wouldn't be his fault. I was a whiz at taking tests but lousy at giving them.

"Sure," he said.

I almost hugged him and it would have been so uncool to let on how excited I was that he'd said yes. So maybe he did like me. I grinned.

"I love pizza. So which place?" he asked.

Or maybe he just wanted the pizza. I really should have given this plan more thought before putting it into action.

To Do List: Read all the Point books!

By Aimee Friedman

- ❏ South Beach
- ❏ French Kiss
- ❏ Hollywood Hills
- ❏ The Year My Sister Got Lucky

- ❏ Airhead
  By Meg Cabot

- ❏ Suite Scarlett
  By Maureen Johnson

- ❏ Love in the Corner Pocket
  By Marlene Perez

- ❏ Hotlanta
  By Denene Millner
  and Mitzi Miller

Summer Boys series by Hailey Abbott

- ❏ Summer Boys
- ❏ Next Summer
- ❏ After Summer
- ❏ Last Summer

In or Out series by Claudia Gabel

- ❏ In or Out
- ❏ Loves Me, Loves Me Not
- ❏ Sweet and Vicious
- ❏ Friends Close, Enemies Closer

- ❏ Orange Is the New Pink
  By Nina Malkin

Making a Splash series by Jade Parker

- ❏ Robyn
- ❏ Caitlin
- ❏ Whitney

Once Upon a Prom series by Jeanine Le Ny

- ❏ Dream
- ❏ Dress
- ❏ Date

PNTLST4